3 - 25 - 2021

"Summer…" Mike said, closing the car door and slipping his hand into hers.

There was that touch, that damned touch. He was a master of making her forget herself with that simple thing. And he would always have that power over her no matter how much she knew she shouldn't let him.

"Let's just get Joe back, then we can think about everything else. As it stands, let's just call a truce. Fair?" From where she stood, it was more than fair—it was a million miles past that given the circumstances. It was better to be a team than it was to fight with the one man whom she had always loved and always would.

He could never know, but it was so easy for him to see if he wanted to—her love for him would always mean sacrifices. Sacrifices she would gladly make if it meant having him in her life.

Thank you to all those who have helped make this book and this series come to life. This has been a fun series to create and see grow and change over time. I hope that these characters and their stories are just as real to you as they are to me.

A special shout-out to my editors and teams at Harlequin and my agent. Your constant and unwavering faith in me is humbling and greatly appreciated.

Also, thank you to Kristin, Clare, Melanie, Herb, Penny, Joe, Mike and Troy. These folks are my behind-the-scenes helpers who help me research, write, edit and even beta read these books at (sometimes) very short notice. To say it takes a village is an understatement!

RESCUE MISSION: SECRET CHILD

DANICA WINTERS

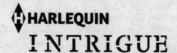

To Jessica—

You are an amazing friend and mother.

Thank you for all you do.

HARLEQUIN®
INTRIGUE®

ISBN-13: 978-1-335-40161-8

Rescue Mission: Secret Child

Copyright © 2021 by Danica Winters

Recycling programs
for this product may
not exist in your area.

This edition published by arrangement with Harlequin Books S.A.

For questions and comments about the quality of this book,
please contact us at CustomerService@Harlequin.com.

Harlequin Enterprises ULC
22 Adelaide St. West, 40th Floor
Toronto, Ontario M5H 4E3, Canada
www.Harlequin.com

Printed in U.S.A.

Danica Winters is a multiple-award-winning, bestselling author who writes books that grip readers with their ability to drive emotion through suspense and occasionally a touch of magic. When she's not working, she can be found in the wilds of Montana, testing her patience while she tries to hone her skills at various crafts—quilting, pottery and painting are not her areas of expertise. She believes the cup is neither half-full nor half-empty, but it better be filled with wine. Visit her website at danicawinters.net.

Books by Danica Winters

Harlequin Intrigue

STEALTH: Shadow Team

A Loaded Question
Rescue Mission: Secret Child

Stealth

Hidden Truth
In His Sights
Her Assassin For Hire
Protective Operation

Mystery Christmas

Ms. Calculation
Mr. Serious
Mr. Taken
Ms. Demeanor

Smoke and Ashes
Dust Up with the Detective
Wild Montana

Visit the Author Profile page at Harlequin.com.

CAST OF CHARACTERS

Mike Spade—Mike has always been quick to feel, fight and make love, and as such, he has made more than his fair share of enemies—including his ex-fiancée, Summer Daniels. Highly trained in cyber tech and surveillance, he and his siblings are part of a special operations team, STEALTH Surveillance.

Summer Daniels—Mike's ex-fiancée and mother of Joseph Spade, Mike's son. With an axe to bury, she will stop at nothing to keep her heart and her child safe. But with her being a double agent for the DTRA, or Defense Threat Reduction Agency, a division within the Pentagon that works to neutralize a variety of cyber, nuclear and terrorist threats, this task force is proving to put everything she holds sacred in danger after their son goes missing.

Joseph "Joe" Spade—Mike and Summer's seven-month-old son, who has a smile as bright and charming as his father's.

Ben Tajir—Summer's rebound man and, conveniently, a fellow agent within Rockwood. As dangerous as he is handsome, he may well be the man behind the kidnapping.

Troy Spade—Mike's brother and a fellow military contractor for the STEALTH Surveillance team.

Zoey Martin—Leader of the STEALTH military contractor group. As smart as she is cold and calculating, she is the linchpin that keeps everything running.

Kevin Warble—Summer's supervisor from within the DTRA.

Rockwood—A corporation with ties to a variety of illegal and nefarious endeavors, including the theft of military weapon–grade secrets from within the USA.

ConFlux—A machining company hired to help engineer and manufacture parts for the different branches of the US military. Their contracts are highly sought after and extremely lucrative, and prove quite the target for their enemies to try to sabotage or steal.

Kate Spade—CEO of ConFlux, a company formerly owned and operated by her parents.

STEALTH—A military contracting group hired for a variety of jobs. Within the organization, Zoey Martin has created the Surveillance team, made up of the six Spade siblings.

Chapter One

There was nothing that Mike hated more than a wedding. It didn't matter whose it was, the season, or the amount of love the happy couple professed to each other. He would still have rather ridden bareback on an angry bull than sit in some kind of mushy gushy feel fest.

Though, when push came to shove, it wasn't the love part that he despised. *Nah.* He had just found there were two events in people's lives that always brought out both the worst and the best from those around them—weddings and funerals.

The last nuptials he had attended had been so filled with poorly masked rancor that by the time the open bar hit, things had turned to verbal tongue-lashings and two brawls. If he hadn't interceded, he was sure a funeral would have soon followed. The last thing he had wanted was to attend two emotionally explosive events that close together.

He definitely would have preferred taking on the bull.

Thinking about bulls, a mechanical bull was exactly what this thing needed to kick it up a notch. He glanced in the direction of the reception hall, a ski lodge just beside the meadow that served as the bunny hill for new skiers in the winter months. Of course, the only thing he could spot through the windows of the A-framed building was a chocolate fountain and a tall, white wedding cake. Nothing gyrating, at least not until his cousin Savannah hit the bottle.

The pastor was talking about the meaning of life or something, but Mike wasn't really listening as he watched the crowd seated in front of him. Aunt Carlene had her signature beehive bun, now sprinkled with a few more gray hairs than when he had last seen her. She'd always been his favorite aunt, and as she and his uncle Bingo sat up at the front on the groom's side in what was traditionally the parents' seats, it made him miss his mom and dad.

Their dad had talked about being at their weddings, a conversation that had always made tears well up in his mother's eyes as she'd wistfully added how she hoped they would all find spouses who helped them be the best versions of themselves. At the time, Mike had teased her and accused her of clearly thinking they all had room for improvement. Of course, she had always waved him off and called him a stinker, but they'd both known what she'd really wanted for him and his five siblings was that they lived lives in which they were truly fulfilled and happy.

When he had gotten engaged to Summer, his

mother had been over the moon. Within a week of finding out his news, she had called Summer and they had already decided on the location, colors and bridal parties. He had still been trying to come to terms with the fact their lives were about to change.

Summer had always been too good for him. She was the kind of woman who was strong and could weather any storm, but she was also the woman who understood that as a military contractor he was cut from a cloth that meant he would never be happy sitting still and would rarely be home. At the time, they had both thought they understood what their lives would entail and had naively believed their love was unlike any other, and that no matter how many horror stories they heard about contractors' relationships falling apart, theirs wouldn't. They had fully bought in to the idea that they, and their relationship, were different.

What idiots they had been.

Many times, like now, when he was forced to go to social functions without a date, his aunt would inevitably try to set him up with someone. He couldn't do it, though. He missed Summer. He missed the way they could just look at one another and know what the other was feeling and thinking.

What they had…it had been something special. But looking back, he wasn't sure they'd been an ideal fit. They were different. She liked hot and he liked cold. He wanted to conquer the world while she wanted to perfect her corner of it. And their biggest difference was their fatal flaw…he wanted all of her heart and she wanted every bit of his soul.

He'd never really get over losing her. Late at night, he would often have to console himself with the thought that, in the end, they had been too young for the kind of commitment they had made to one another. Who could promise forever when they weren't even sure where in the world they would be tomorrow?

She had deserved better. He should have answered her calls after they'd broken things off, but some things were just too damn hard.

In front of him at the altar, the bride, Kate Scot, slipped the wedding band on his brother's finger as she smiled up at him and said her vows. There was no mention of her obeying his brother and Mike had to hold back his chuckle. Summer had always protested that particular vow, as well. He and his brother Troy had always had a similar taste for independent women.

He had to get his mind off Summer or he would only swirl further into madness, madness that would lead to far too much beer and he'd be the one who'd end up dancing with his gyrating cousin.

Nope. He couldn't get himself roped into any of that kind of nonsense. He had a stoic, lone-wolf reputation to uphold.

As soon as Kate and Troy kissed, he got up from his chair and moved steadily away from the crowd, not so fast to give his retreat away, but quickly enough to get out of the melee of family members who would try to rope him into a conversation. He'd dropped the gift off and watched the I do's, the rest he could hear about later.

He had parked at the far end of the lot, nose out in case he had to make a quick escape. But as he approached his truck, he noticed a woman standing near the tailgate. She had her back to him, looking toward the timber like there were answers in the pines. The only thing she would find by standing so close to his truck was a problem.

"Can I help you?" he asked, hoping the woman was just someone like him, trying to escape the ceremony, rather than a spook up to no good. In his business, he had to view everyone as a potential threat.

The woman turned around and, as she did, their eyes met. Those green eyes. Those eyes, the vibrant, down-to-earth color of spring moss, had always had the power to weave right into his soul. They, and the woman they belonged to, had an unspeakable gift to sparkle with contagious joy and instantly darken when danger beckoned. A thousand words were not enough to explain all the things her eyes had conveyed to him over the years; in fact, no words created could elicit the same feelings that she could with a simple glance.

A hint of a smile flickered over her features as she looked at him, her eyes lighting up, but just as quickly as the light had come, it disappeared and was replaced with pure unadulterated hate. Sadly, he understood why and how confused she must have been feeling, and a guilty sadness filled him. He had done this to her. He'd had a hand in the look she was sending him and the woman she had become.

"I'm sorry." It was the only thing he could think to say. As soon as it left his lips, he wished he'd led with something more innocuous, maybe a hello instead. Yet, the milk was spilled.

She chuckled. Blading her feet, she turned slightly away from him. He didn't blame her for not wanting to look at him a second longer than necessary. Then again, she knew this was his truck... She must have been waiting for him.

"I was hoping you would be here." He surprised himself with those words. If anything, he had feared seeing her—seeing her only made everything rise to the surface.

"We both know that's not true. I'm the last person you wanted to have be here."

Ouch.

Sighing, he tried to quell the ache that had suddenly filled his entire being. If he wasn't careful, this would only lead to a fight; they had one hell of a track record in bringing animosity out in one another.

"You were waiting for me?" he asked, trying to keep the question inquisitive instead of kindling for her rage.

She sat on the bumper of his truck, covering her chest with her arms and protecting her core. He'd seen her take this position a thousand times, and none had ever turned out well.

"I'm not here because I really want to be, let me start by saying that."

He had no doubt, but he wasn't about to say that aloud, so he simply nodded, waiting for her to continue.

"I was in the city for work. Ran into Kate and she invited me. I figured I needed to be here to show my support. Troy was always a good man." She paused, like she wanted him to respond, but he was far too gun-shy.

He had a number of things he wanted to ask her, starting with how her life was going. The last time he had spoken to her, she had been employed by a contracting company, running intel.

"Still working with STRIKE?" he asked.

She gave him a sidelong look, but she didn't answer at first, as if she was checking to see if he knew about the company; and if he did, what his opinion was. He gave her nothing, though he'd heard all about the company. They had made waves by controlling American gas reserves on military bases, gas that had lost thousands of barrels along the railways between bases and even more in the pipelines leading into the American strongholds. "Still working intel?" he asked, trying again.

She nodded. "Yes. By the way, I heard about you and your brother's run-in with Rockwood."

It had only been a couple of months since he had found his ass getting shot at in the streets of downtown Missoula—after the group had worked to take down Kate's family's company from the inside out—but it already felt like ancient history. "Yep, it's how Kate and Troy met. Never thought things would move this fast between them. You know Troy, he's typically about the speed of cold molasses."

"No," Summer said with a laugh, "that's you."

He felt the lash. "Slow is smooth and smooth is fast."

"You can try to feed me all that nonsense if you want, but you and I both know that you are never one to jump into or out of anything without a hell of a lot of thought—thoughts that you generally forget to express to others."

This time the whip struck faster, harder, and the lashes cut deeper with their truths.

"I'm sorry."

"You said that." She sounded almost glib. "It doesn't change the fact that you did what you did. And you are going to have to forgive the fact that I may never get over how badly you hurt me. Move on, sure. Move forward, you know it. But hurt...*forever.*"

"I know." He stared down at the toes of the wing tips his brother had asked him to wear for pictures, wishing he had stayed for the reception instead of trying to find any kind of refuge away from the crowds. They would have been a hell of a lot easier to deal with than this. "I hurt, too, Summer. It was never my intention to—"

She put a stop to his talking with the wave of her hand. "I didn't mean to take things this direction. The past is the past. Let's leave it there."

He didn't dare to believe she was done talking

about their shared history, but he was glad for the parley. "Done. Now, what do you need?" If there was anything he could do to get back in her good graces, he would.

"Who said I needed anything?"

"I know you're friends with my brother and Kate, but we both know this kind of thing isn't your scene." He shrugged, making her smirk.

He had loved that guilty smile.

There was so much he missed about her and so many things he wished he could just tell her… Like the fact he would never stop loving her. He just hadn't been ready to walk down the aisle. Maybe he would never be ready for a real relationship. Marriage meant putting her in danger, and he was a protector at his core; a job that required he focus on things bigger than himself. The only way he could do that was by being selfless and giving up what he loved the most.

"I am here for them…and I don't hate weddings, even though…" She brushed the rest of the sentence away like it was some kind of pestering fly. "I did have something I wanted to talk to you about."

He didn't want to talk about work, but he had a feeling that was exactly where she was going to try to take things since she had brought up his and Troy's run-in with Rockwood. He was especially attuned to subtle snooping, and the fact that she'd asked about his recent job put him on edge. "STEALTH's work for ConFlux is strictly confidential. As much as I would like to help you out, you know how it is."

"Kate said your team would be who I needed to talk to about the security breach. That you could give me information."

"The way I see it, there are a few things wrong with this, Summer. First, I'm not the guy you want to be talking to if you want answers about this. And second, who is to say the people at STRIKE are people who can be trusted?"

She slid him a sly smile. She was hiding something, but he didn't know exactly what. "You know I'd never be a part of anything I hadn't vetted. My team is with the good guys gang, same as your teams at STEALTH. We work for the greater good."

She could do all the vetting she wanted, but that didn't mean she saw everything or had come to all the right conclusions. And when it came to the *greater good*, they both knew that was a load of nonsense.

"As far as I'm concerned, whatever was stolen from ConFlux is between them and the federal acronyms they are working for and with. If you stick your nose too deep into this kind of warfare, you will lose your face. Be careful, Summer." He turned as he moved to retreat.

"Stop," she called after him. "I have one more thing…"

He halted and faced her. "If this is about your work, as much as I want to, I can't help you. I'm out, Summer."

"I know, and that's fine. But my work isn't why I'm really here." She paused, chewing on her bottom

lip as she clicked on her phone. "I have something—
someone actually—you need to meet." She lifted her
phone and he had to step closer to see the picture.

Smiling up at him was a baby. He had big blue
eyes and appeared to be giggling at something off-
screen.

"This is Joseph. I call him Joe." There was a soft
cadence to her voice, an unmistakable tenderness
that came when a mother looked upon her child. "Joe
is our son."

Chapter Two

Summer really hadn't intended to tell Mike about the baby this way. There was such a deep, aching sadness in Mike's features, she wanted to wrap her arms around him. To bury her face in his chest and say how sorry she was. How she had wanted to give him the news for so long; how many times she had tried to call. She moved toward him, but stopped her advance.

Wait. No. She wasn't the one who needed to feel bad about how this had all played out. This was on him.

She had called. She had tried to contact him. *He* was the one who had refused to talk to her, to take her calls. And telling a man he was going to be a father wasn't something that anyone should do over a voice mail or a text. If he was upset, then he could only be upset with himself. He had been the weakling who couldn't face her after he had broken her heart.

Sucking in a long inhale, she collected herself.

Life had a dark sense of humor.

"You named him Joe?" Mike's voice cracked, breaking away some of her anger.

She nodded. "Joseph. After your dad. I thought it was only right."

Mike had never been one to cry, not even when he had told her that he wasn't going to marry her...right in the middle of the makeshift bridal suite twenty minutes before their wedding was set to begin. The church had started to fill with their guests, and the caterers and florists had everything in place. When he'd spoken those words, those heartbreaking words, *I can't... I can't be your forever*, the string quartet had been playing "Ave Maria." Ever since, she had hated that song; before it had been one of her absolute favorites. But that day, there were many things she had thought she would love forever that had turned to ash in her mouth.

It was crazy how, in a single moment, everything in a life could change.

"Can I see the picture again?" He sounded plaintive, as if unsure she'd agree, his voice soft, even wavering.

She noted the way he didn't say *his* picture. It was *the* picture. As if the baby whom her whole life now revolved around was simply an image, nothing more. But then again, she had no doubt she was gunning for a fight. For the last few weeks, she had been trying to imagine every possible outcome of this meeting, but every scenario she had imagined had ended with a fight. No matter how badly she wanted things to be amicable between them, her pain was likely to stand in the way.

She pulled up Joe's picture and handed her phone over to Mike. He stared at the screen and there was a well of tears growing in his eyes. Would he let them fall?

Regardless of her personal feelings, they had a child together. A child who deserved to know his father and his entire family; even if that family wasn't really hers. Regardless of her feelings for him, Mike deserved to have a chance...a chance he didn't have to take, a chance he didn't have to grasp with both hands. More, he deserved to have a *choice*, one that didn't include her getting in his way or keeping his child from him.

Though she hated him for what he had done to her and the way he had made her feel, there was no doubt there was still a part of her that loved him, and would always love him. That part of her soul was deep, and she would have to keep it buried, but only love could make her feel this confused and so up in the air.

"He is so handsome. How old is he?"

"Seven months, yesterday. He has started to crawl and is starting to get into everything. He loves to be at my feet when I'm working in the kitchen." A smile took over her entire being as she thought about Joe's tiny fingers against her skin and the feel of picking him up and putting him on her hip, laughing as she moved. "He has a laugh that can light up the world. You'd love it." There was a bright timbre in her voice that made her wish she hadn't spoken the last bit aloud.

Mike nodded and there was a strained silence between them. She cleared her throat, knowing he could outwait her in any uncomfortable situation; it was basically one of his many superpowers.

"He is staying with my friend Jessica right now."

"Ah," he said, nodding as he looked down at Joe's picture. "So, you are still living in Great Falls?"

She wasn't really living anywhere, but she didn't want to admit to him that her new job was keeping her from being the mom she had always wanted to be. Yet, survival and putting food on the table were forcing her to make choices she'd never thought she would have to make.

"Right now, I'm staying in Missoula. Doing some training and certification courses, then I'm going to head back up to the high-line."

He nodded, but she could read the many thoughts flickering out and over his features, and yet, he still said nothing. His silence was going to be the death of her.

"Jess has been really good with him. She is such a good godmother."

"I bet," he said, his words filled with a pain that spilled over and poured straight to her core.

"If you want, you could come and meet him. You are welcome anytime."

A smile stretched over his lips, but there was a tiredness in his eyes. "I'd love that. To meet him, that is. When works for you?"

Oh, she had walked right into that. Of course, he would want to see their son this very minute. If she had been in his position, she would have wanted the same thing. Yet she couldn't drop everything and make the three-hour trip to Great Falls, spend the night, and then make the same trip back.

Her bosses wouldn't allow her to just arbitrarily take time off.

Then again, this could be turned into a positive. If anything, this was the perfect opportunity to bring her and Mike closer; and maybe she could get him to open up to her a little bit. She could see if she could mine some more information about Rockwood for her team at the DTRA—the Defense Threat Reduction Agency, a division of the Pentagon's Defense Advanced Research Projects Agency, also known as DARPA.

She would have to make a few phone calls, but maybe her boss would go along with this idea. Heck, she could even play it off like this had been her plan all along. Though she couldn't have predicted this any more than she could predict the nature of the wind. Just when she thought she understood the man she had once promised her future to, he would swirl away and carry her dreams off with him.

"If you wanted, I have to button a few things and then head up in a couple of days. You can follow me up, or whatever."

His brows rose, like he was surprised she would suggest they take separate cars for the long drive. He shouldn't have been. As much as she wanted to ply him for information about their teams' common enemy, the last thing she wanted was for them to be in such close proximity without a clearly defined exit. She needed to be careful around him; he always had a way of pulling her back in even when everything inside her shouted for her to stay away. Come hell or high water, this time she was going to listen to the little voice that told her to be wary when it came to any kind of relationship with this man—even a relationship of convenience.

"I have to work," he said, looking back in the direction of the chalet where the reception was now in full swing.

Okay, so maybe he didn't need to see his son just this minute. Work, once again, came first.

Even from where she stood, she could make out the sounds of someone making a speech and a round of applause.

That should have been their moment. And yet here they were, once again, standing so close to happiness that they could almost taste it, but still a world apart. She was fated to starve in a world filled with tasty morsels of happiness. Ah, the irony.

"If you wanted, I could go in there and talk to whomever I needed to talk to. Who's your team leader? I bet if I explain the circumstances, some allowances can be made."

He gave her a surprised look, like he thought she was calling his bluff in some way. "Do you really want to go in there?" He nudged his chin in the direction of the party.

Anywhere had to be better than standing there, alone with him and forced to face their uncomfortable reality.

"I could use some chicken or fish." She patted her belly. The action was oddly familiar and, as she moved, he smiled.

"When aren't you hungry?" Mike chuckled.

Right after a breakup, she thought, but she didn't dare say the words aloud. She simply walked past him and toward the reception.

There were two seats in the corner, and for once she had wished there'd been assigned tables so she wouldn't have been forced to sit next to him.

Guests enjoyed the buffet, and the entire simple and pioneer-style wedding spoke of Troy. Kate must have been just like the man she married, and the realization made her instantly like the woman. Summer had always loved the entire Spade family, even AJ, who, as the family patriarch, always seemed to have a spine welded out of steel.

AJ was sitting at Troy's side, the only groomsman in the wedding party. Kate's sister was sitting beside her, wearing a blue dress that looked as beautiful with its A-line waist as it was comfortable. Yep, Summer definitely liked her; this woman that could have been her sister-in-law if only Summer had played her cards right. Summer should have known that getting married was the one thing that Mike feared above anything else.

He had always talked about how much he hated the entire institution and the symbolic ownership that came with the arrangement. Ownership was slavery and, regardless of who owned whom, freedom was something he would forever lay down his life to protect.

And while he had remained free—thanks to his actions—her heart would never be freely given again. It would always be chained to the past.

They moved through the buffet line, putting together their plates of food, and they made small talk as they went to the table. Servers came around with drinks and after she'd had a beer and he'd had two, the conversation between them started to become a little looser, easier as they slipped back into their old ways.

As they talked, the world around them slowly began to disappear. More and more people moved to the dance floor as the DJ played the worst and best of all wedding songs. Right now, the chicken dance was blaring and even the older folks were out on the cedar floor, flapping their arms like makeshift wings.

"You want to dance?" Mike asked, motioning toward the craziness on display in front of them.

She didn't answer right away; instead she watched Troy, who was laughing as he waddled around his bride like a teetering bird. Oh, it was going to be a long, drunken night. Under no circumstances could she fall into some old habits…habits that led her toward the bedroom with Mike.

He was off-limits. He'd hurt her too bad.

And yet, as he slipped his hand around hers and helped her to her feet and then to the dance floor, his touch was like a salve on the burn of their past.

Chapter Three

In a million years, Mike would have never thought his life would make a complete about-face in just a matter of hours.

The morning after the wedding, he walked down the hallway that led to his bedroom at the Widow Maker Ranch, STEALTH's headquarters, and he peered through the crack in the door. Summer was stretched out across his bed as if she owned the place. Her dark hair was haloed around her head and her arms were up, giving her a look as if she was floating in a pool of water.

He had always loved to watch her sleep. She was serene and, for once in her life, she looked at peace with the world around her.

With Joe in the picture now, he couldn't help but wonder when was the last time she had actually had a good night's sleep.

Learning about Joe had been a gut punch. He wanted to be angry at her for not telling him sooner about the baby, but he couldn't be...not when he thought of all the phone calls he had gotten from her, phone calls he had sent straight to voice mail. This wasn't her fault. He was the jerk, the weaker one, because he couldn't face her. This was on him. And now he was going to have to make things right. At the very least, he would try.

He had already missed seeing the ultrasound and hearing the baby's heartbeat for the first time. He had missed holding Summer's hand while she went to her prenatal appointments and learned about the sex of the baby. He had missed watching his son come into the world and take his first breath. More, he had missed supporting the woman he had once pledged his life.

Though things had gone well between them last night. They had spent the night dancing and laughing during wedding—his cousin Savannah had been even more wild than he'd anticipated, getting up on the wedding party's table at one point—but the night had ended with him pouring Summer into his bed and her whispering a series of simple words that he would never forget. "I'll never forgive you. You left me... *Us.*"

No doubt, she wouldn't recall what she had told him, but he would. Beer had been the truth serum that had unlocked what had been hidden in her heart.

If he had a choice, he would vow to never leave her adrift again. No matter what she or Joe needed, he would provide it; all while keeping his heart out of the mix. Old feelings would complicate things, open wounds. If he was going to be able to stay in their lives, he couldn't risk losing them for any reason—and especially one as selfish as love.

Summer shifted in the bed and looked over in his direction through a squinted eye. "How long have you been there?" she asked, her voice raspy from sleep.

So much for being stealthy. He opened up the door a tiny bit more. "I was just walking by, thought I'd check in on you. Need anything? Water? Pain meds?"

She groaned slightly as she stretched and must have done a mental inventory of what exactly had gone on last night. "I'd ask if we…*you know*…but—"

"You know my hard pass on any woman who isn't in control. And last night, you were well out of control." He sent her a soft, understanding smile. "Besides, you made it abundantly clear you were not interested in me—or any man *until the end of time*." He made air quotes as he recited her words back to her.

She shoved her face into the pillow, not bothering to deny her boycott of relationships.

Oddly enough, he found the idea of her not dating anyone—even him—reassuring. Though he didn't have a shot with her, ever, at least they could be alone together. Though, in all truth, she deserved to be happy and find love with a man who would treat her like the princess she was.

"See you in a few?" he asked, and when she nodded, he went downstairs for breakfast.

Twenty minutes later, she was fresh-faced after a shower. She walked into the kitchen, grabbed a cup of coffee and her keys and started outside. "Coming? It's a long drive to Great Falls," she said, not looking back at him.

"What?" he called after her. Last night she had said that it would take her a few days to get things lined up with her work, that she couldn't just drop everything and take him to see his son. And yet, she was now tearing out of the house like her feet were on fire.

Whatever, he wasn't going to look this gift horse in the mouth.

Luckily, his family and the rest of the crews were in the main house, or they would have had a ball ribbing him for Summer coming home with him. As it was, he was surprised he wasn't getting a slew of texts after the dancing and frivolity last night. Maybe they were all too hungover to be too full of snark this morning; regardless, it was only a matter of time until a few of them started asking questions. Especially after the conversation he'd had with Zoey Martin, their STEALTH boss, telling her that he was going to need a couple of weeks off so he could go meet his son.

Oh, that tidbit of information was going to sweep through the family like wildfire.

He really needed to stop going to weddings.

He stood and, grabbing his coat and a travel mug of coffee, he made his way outside after Summer. She was standing beside her car. "Do I want to know how we got home last night?" she asked, nudging her chin in the direction of his pickup.

"No worries, I went out this morning with AJ and we got your car. No drinking and driving." His hard pass on drunken anything ran the gamut.

"So, AJ knows I came back here…with you… And…" She gave a resigned sigh. "Crap."

"You know AJ, he isn't going to say anything to anyone," he said, walking over toward his truck.

"Where are you going?" Summer called after him.

"I thought you said we weren't going to drive together?" he asked, confused by her about-face.

"Saves gas if we just go together."

He had never known Summer to turn on a dime, but maybe she had changed more than even he could understand since the last time he had spoken with her. From what he'd been told, motherhood changed a person. In the few hours since he'd found out he was a father, he could feel himself changing too. Suddenly, his life had taken on a new meaning and a fight he hadn't known he'd had within him—he would do anything for this boy whom he had never met. He would give his life. He couldn't even begin to imagine the transformation in Summer, one she'd gone through alone because of his failure to respond to her. His chest ached.

He would understand if she never forgave him for his missteps in life. He doubted he would ever forgive himself.

As he got into her car, he peeked into the back seat. He expected to find a car seat base or something to give her role as a mother away, but it was conspicuously devoid of any whispers of a child.

He could understand it, though, her need to keep her personal life out of any sort of public view. In their line of work, private lives were weak points. That was part of the reason he had told himself he couldn't get married. If they had...they would both have been weakened. Others could have used their love against them.

The first hour of the drive, they sat in silence as he waited for her to start talking. They careened through the mountains, the timber flashing by as they rolled past pristine rivers and blue skies. The snow was gone from the mountains, but there was still an icy chill in the air. When the peaks finally gave way to rolling plains, it was as if the mask of the mountains had lifted and so had Summer's mood.

Finally, she looked over at him. "I told Jess we were coming, she said she would be around with Joe anytime. I think she is looking forward to getting a bit of a break. She has had him for the last week."

"I'm excited to meet him. Seriously." He wanted to ask her how often she left Joe in Jessica's care, but he didn't want to come off sounding judgmental in any way, so he remained quiet. Tension reverberated through the air as it was; he didn't need to add more. "And I'm glad Jess has been so great."

"I'm glad she is so willing to help me out. I have come to really understand the adage that it takes a village to raise a child."

"Well, I hope you know that I'm more than happy to help in any way I can. I want to be a part of your support system. Money, housing...whatever."

She gave him a sidelong glance, like she was looking for the truth in his words.

"I mean it," he repeated. "And I'm not going to say it again, but I want you to know that I will always be sorry for how things played out between us."

She raised her hand, silencing him. "Let's not talk about it. What happened… Not anymore… We have more pressing things to deal with and if we go there, ever…well, it's not good for either one of us."

He nodded, agreeing. There was no fixing the past. "Here's to moving forward." He raised his coffee mug in salute.

She smiled, and the simple action lifted the heaviness that had blanketed him. Maybe there was some kind of hope for a budding friendship, after all.

Twenty miles and a pit stop later, she let him take over driving. She stared out the window as he drove the straight, long road that led to the north. He'd always hated this drive. Many people thought of the rolling prairie as beautiful in its languid hills and lolling grains, but he found it monotonous. The only thing that changed was the crops. Though, maybe it wasn't the prairie that was at fault; maybe he had too many mountainous ridges and sharp crags around his soul.

Regardless of where he was in Montana, at least he was in the state he called home. These roads, these mountains, hills and valleys were where he wanted to be forever. He'd spent far too many days overseas and in foreign lands longing for this place to take it for granted.

"Do you miss it?" she asked.

"Huh? What?"

"Now that you are working in surveillance, do you miss your old job gunning down bad guys?" She was staring at him.

"I forgot how well you can read my thoughts." He chuckled, trying to dispel some of the pressure of her question.

"It's in your face. You always get that look when you're thinking about the Sandbox, it's like you're a million miles away."

He pinched his lips as he nodded. "I always thought I had a good poker face."

"Maybe you do, but you will never have one when it comes to me."

And that right there was one of the reasons he had forgotten—until now—that he had fallen in love with her. She seemed to see him in a way that no one else in the world ever would.

"Do you like the work you are doing with STEALTH?" she asked.

"Yeah, you know me. I'm happier working in the shadows, and the team lets me do that."

She laughed. "I hear you there. Lately, I've been working more in the open and I have to say that I miss the old days when I worked more behind a desk."

"So, you don't like your new job?"

She shrugged. "It's fine. But they are asking things of me that I'm not loving."

He didn't dare to question her about what in her

job she didn't enjoy. Those kinds of conversations, in their lines of work, were places they could never go.

"I heard about the shooting at ConFlux. I'm glad you made it out unscathed. Did they ever find the shooter?"

He glanced over at her, surprised that she would press anything work-related. "We got as far as we could with the information we had. As far as I know, the feds are still digging into that one. And us talking about my job? I'm done. I told you before, this isn't something I'm going to open up about, especially when we don't even play for the same teams." He tried to ignore the way his hackles rose. Summer was someone he could trust and yet his professional instincts kept him silent on any details related to STEALTH jobs.

She huffed. "And I told you that we're playing for the same team."

He opened his mouth to challenge her, but she didn't pause long enough.

"But I respect your need for privacy. If I was your boss, I would be proud of you for your hard line on this. You are the kind of employee I strive to be."

Did that mean she had secrets she wanted to tell him? Was there something she needed help with, but was too afraid to ask?

"Are you okay, Summer? Safe?" Sometimes he hated the way they had to speak in the nuanced code that came with their lifestyle.

Her hands tightened into balls in her lap; he'd stumbled onto something. But what?

She chewed on her lip, but she didn't respond.

Silence rolled by along with the miles until the grain silos and hotels marking the Great Falls skyline came into view. Pointing to the upcoming exit, she gave him a few simple directions toward Jess's house. The home was a simple box-style, as if built in the 1950s when resources were limited and people only built exactly what they could pay for out of pocket and with little residual expense.

As he pulled to a stop, Summer finally turned to him. "Mike, I won't compromise you or your job, but I could use your help."

He would give her anything. There was so much he needed to make up for. But he could never compromise his teams—not even for her. And sometimes even letting out a small seemingly inconsequential bit of info could put a colleague in jeopardy.

Yet maybe there was something he could do to help, something he was sure wouldn't put a single life in peril. "What, exactly, do you need?"

"I need to find out what you know about Rockwood."

"Why?"

She shook her head, refusing to give him more. "If I tell you, I'm as good as dead."

His hackles rose even more. "If you don't tell me exactly what the hell is going on, there is nothing I can do to help you. You can't give me half-truths. It's all or nothing, Summer."

The front door of the little thrifty-looking house opened. Jessica stepped out, her blond hair whipping around her face as she lifted the little boy's chunky arm and helped him to wave at them.

He was upset with Summer, but as soon as he saw the sweet, cherubic cheeks of the little blond boy in Jessica's arms, he forgot about everything but the baby. This boy, this little ball of chunk.

He stepped out of the car, slipping the keys in his pocket as he rushed toward the front steps. Summer exited the vehicle and he could make out the sound of her laughing softly behind him.

Walking up the sidewalk to his son, he could feel a single tear slip down his cheek.

As he approached, the little boy smiled and wiggled in Jessica's arms. He thrust out his arms, surprising Mike in the way he motioned for him, a stranger.

Jessica sent him a warm smile as she lifted Joe up and handed the baby over.

As he took him, he smiled through the tears that streaked his face.

This. This moment was what his entire life had led up to.

This angel was his now, and forever more, his everything.

Chapter Four

Watching him with their son drew memories to the front of Summer's mind, memories she had believed long forgotten. As Joe touched his face and giggled, then coyly tucked his face in Mike's neck, the simple innocent action reminded Summer of the first time Mike had made her laugh. She couldn't remember the exact joke—some dad joke about bees—but she could still remember the flames of love that had burned away her mask and exposed the real her.

She had thought herself capable of compartmentalizing love from work. And yet now, standing there and watching the two men who had brought so much joy to her life, she knew there was no such thing as compartmentalizing, not really. Sure, a person could shift attention and focus, stuffing away inconvenient feelings, but in life's quiet moments, those truths always returned...with more pain than any type of physical injury. Though she couldn't go back in time and make different choices, she could learn from them. And her greatest lesson to date? Love was a weakness.

Mike looked over his shoulder at her, his cheek damp. Had this man, this chiseled-from-granite man, really shed a tear?

Her weakness for him rippled through her like a piece had broken from his hard façade and dropped into the lake of her life.

Allergies. He had to be suffering from allergies.

"You didn't tell me he was so freaking cute." He glanced back at the boy. "He has your eyes."

"And your nose," she said, walking over and giving Joe a little bop to the round tip.

He giggled as she smiled down at him, making funny faces and blowing raspberries.

Mike looked up at Jessica. "It's nice to see you. Been a long time."

Even though she had warned her friend that Mike would be coming with her to Great Falls to meet his son, Jess looked at Summer like she wasn't entirely sure how she should respond to the interloper on her doorstep. Summer gave her a faint nod, hoping it would show her that this was all okay, this was what needed to happen for everything to fall into place.

Jess composed herself and plastered a smile on her lips as she moved her gaze to Mike. "I'm glad you are here. Joe has been waiting to meet you."

There was a pained expression on Mike's face, as though Jess's words were some sort of razor wire that had wrapped around him, piercing him with each syllabic burst.

"I would have come sooner, but…well, you know…" He cleared his throat.

"Let's not worry about the past," Summer said, walking by him and waving off his discomfort like it wasn't going to haunt him.

She didn't need a reminder of the pain that would always rest between them.

Jess followed her in, letting Mike stand alone with the boy for a moment before walking into the house behind them.

"Want some coffee? Tea?" Jess asked, giving Summer a pointed look.

Jess wanted to meet with her alone in the kitchen. Sometimes she hated having a friend who could speak through only a glance.

"I'd take a glass of water, you know me…nothing too fancy." Mike smiled, but he didn't look away from Joe.

There was no doubt Mike was just as much in love with his son as she was.

Jessica's living room looked like something off Pinterest with its cute farmhouse-chic décor and earthy tones. Everything was in its place, not even a speck of dust on a single surface. For a woman who spent her days working as an analyst for the FBI, Jessica always impressed Summer with her ability to keep things spotless as well as lend a helping hand with Joe. Summer could barely keep up with her job in intel, let alone be perfect in every other facet of her life.

The kitchen was an extension of the rest of the

pristine house; even the flour container was perfectly centered and devoid of any residue.

One day, maybe, she would be able to keep a house like that of her friend. Then again, she could barely keep her car clean.

"Thanks for watching Joe. I hope he was good for you." Summer walked to the cupboard and pulled out a bottle and a can of formula. "Did you have enough of everything while I was gone?"

Jessica nodded. "You know Joe, all he wants to do is make everyone smile around him. And I had more than enough of everything, no worries. You done training? It go well?"

For a split second, Summer wondered what *it* Jessica was talking about—her meetings for work or her seeing Mike. Of all the possible meanings, she chose the one that would be the least uncomfortable to talk about.

"Work was good. We weren't buttoned up, but after I talked to the higher-ups, they decided I needed to handle things here and waved me through."

No doubt, given Jess's work in acronyms, she knew there was far more about Summer's work in Missoula than she was telling her—thankfully, Jess didn't press for answers.

Ah, it was great to have a friend who just *got it*.

Jess nodded, like she could hear all the things Summer wasn't saying. "So, we gonna talk about the big, burly elephant who is standing in the middle of my living room?"

"I would call him a jackass, but if you want to talk about him…ask away."

Jess laughed, grabbing the pitcher from the fridge and setting it out to get him a glass of water. "How did it go?"

"Fine. Better than expected."

Jessica nodded. "Did you guys discuss a parenting plan? Does he want to get back together?"

"Geez, Jess. He's only known about Joe for a matter of hours. Don't you think you're getting a little ahead of yourself?"

Jess turned and faced her. "You know you have thought through all of these things, probably a thousand times faster and more often than I have. You have to have some kind of idea how he is going to work through all of this. You know him."

Correction, she *had* known him. Or rather, she had thought she had known him. And yet Mike always had a way of surprising her at the most inopportune times.

"I'm sure he is going to want to get some sort of parenting plan sorted out, but his life is generally even more all over the map than mine." Summer moved to the sink, filling the bottle with water and adding the powdered formula. Shaking it, she thought of his time in Syria, working with STEALTH. There were weeks in which she had not been able to hear his voice and had barely gotten more than a sentence or two in messages.

Though he was now working a different job for

the company, it didn't mean he would be at home that much more. And how could a man who had no stability in his personal life be able to be a father?

It struck her that maybe that was the reason Mike had left her…maybe he had been right in his assessment of his life. Maybe he really wasn't able to be her everything—even if they loved one another. Hell, what if he had been right?

If that were true, perhaps it had been a mistake to tell him about Joe. This would put a whole hell of a lot more pressure on him—and her. He had crumpled under the possibility of being a husband. How would he respond when it came to feeling the burden of being a father?

There was a wail as Joe's cry filled the air.

What if she was making a huge mistake? This telling him about Joe and bringing him here without their thinking about all the potential consequences for both of them… All of it… She should have stayed silent, stayed home, stayed in the shadows.

Why did doing the right thing have to feel so wrong? It would have been so much easier to just let things remain as they had been, her blaming him for leaving her and their son, and then resenting him for the mistakes he hadn't known he had made.

Then again, telling him wasn't entirely about him.

She would be lying if she tried to say that it was all about Joe, either.

This was all too much about her and her needs, both personal and professional.

She needed answers for work and she needed to get the cloud of secrets out of her head. Now that the truth of Joe was out in the open, she didn't have to be caught up in the whirlwind of questions anymore. Now they could deal with the hurricane as it came.

Joe's crying intensified and, shaking the bottle, she walked out to the living room. "You want to feed him? I bet he is just hungry." Mike looked even more upset than Joe did, even with his little chubby red cheeks and tears. In fact, Mike's face was so pinched and tense that it made her wonder if he had some-how hurt himself in the few moments she had been in the kitchen.

"Are you okay?" she asked, not waiting for him to answer.

"I'm fine. Just hand me that bottle," he said, shoving out his hand like the bottle was the pin that could be put back into the grenade.

She bit back a chuckle as she gave him the bottle.

When Mike stuck it in Joe's mouth, the baby started to suckle so hard that there were audible gulps as he swallowed the milk. Though she was aware such a greedy feeding would lead to a gassy tummy, she still loved that sound. It was as if it thrummed some primal motherly chord, the music of fulfilling her baby's needs and helping him to grow. The timbre of success and pride. Making it even better was that it was coming from her baby in his father's arms.

Their family was whole. Their village was strong.

Instinct screamed that this, this was what Joe needed.

And yet, logically, that wasn't true. They had been doing fine on their own. She was a strong, independent woman.

She readjusted her footing, straightening her back with pride and consternation.

Mike loved this baby, but if he walked out and left them, she would be fine. *They* would be fine. The world would keep on going with or without him.

"Here, why don't you let me take him?" she asked, moving to take the baby.

"No, I got him. Really," Mike said, moving Joe away from her.

She had to check the anger that boiled up within her. Maybe she was being irrational and thinking too much; getting upset with him for this simple action would only lead to a fight. That wasn't what any of them needed. Not now, not ever. At least, not really.

What she needed was an ally, a friend, and a father. He could be all of those things; she would just need to check herself and allow him to be them.

This was going to be so much harder than she had ever imagined.

She dropped her arms to her sides.

Let him do this, she thought. *Let him be Joe's father.*

There was no going back on the choices either one of them had made; he had chosen to leave and she had chosen to bring him back into their lives. The only option was for them to move forward together in whatever way they needed to be for Joe to have the support systems and family that would bring him comfort and success as he grew up.

Joe needed this.

And truth be told, so did she. She *needed* them to be a family.

Chapter Five

Joe was nestled into the car seat in the back as they drove to Summer's apartment. The only sound was of the road and the occasional happy squeaks of the baby playing. Mike could get used to that.

"If you want, I can put you up in a hotel. We could both stay there." Summer shifted uncomfortably in her seat as she drove.

"You don't want me at your place?"

"Well... It's not that, it's just...well, it's not exactly put together right now." She sounded nervous, but he couldn't tell if it was because they were going to be staying another night so close to one another or if it was actually because of the state of her place.

"You know I've spent more than my fair share of nights in Connexes with dozens of other dudes. My standards for sleep and comfort are pretty low."

She laughed, releasing some of the tension. "You have me there."

"Besides," he continued, "I have no room to judge you for your accommodations. I'm the one holing up in my company's ranch. I don't even have an apartment to call my own."

"You were never one to be strapped down."

There was a needle in her voice and it made him wonder if she had meant for it to be there or if it had just been a convenient jab, one she couldn't miss the chance for taking.

"You know my world. Any day could be my last."

"Mmm-hmm," she said, a dark expression settling on her face like a shadow. "I always hated when you talked like that."

If he wasn't careful, this could lead to an argument. They had been down this road so many times. Yet he couldn't just let her comment go without some sort of response. If he did, she would get to the fight all by herself, anyway.

"You know how it can be." He paused. "Luckily, this new job with STEALTH has me mostly working in the States. For now, at the very least." Though he had meant it to assuage some of the anger and perhaps trepidation she was feeling, the look on her face didn't change. Her eyes were still dark and solidly focused on the road.

She was definitely gearing up for combat. He couldn't let things go in that direction.

"I think it's great that you are working with STRIKE. I've heard good things."

She chuffed, but *that* look disappeared. It was replaced by something more stoic, less readable. "They are a good company. They have good goals at heart, but I'm sure things are a bit different than they are at STEALTH. STRIKE was very much about the bottom line."

"It sounds like there is something there, something you are resenting."

She jerked, looking over at him. Clearly, he'd struck a nerve.

"That's not what I was saying at all. I'm just saying they aren't a family-run company. STRIKE is all about measurable and marketable achievement."

"And they have you feeling pressured?" he pressed.

Her hands tightened on the steering wheel and her jaw clenched. "If you don't want to tell me anything about Rockwood, that's fine. But I'm not going to sit here and allow you to grill me."

Yep, she was definitely looking for a fight. But why? What was she hiding? What was she hoping to get him to do for her?

"Look, Summer, I don't want to argue with you. I want us to get along, especially now that Joe is in the picture," he said, glancing back at the baby, though all he could see was the back of the car seat.

She sucked in a long breath. "I wasn't looking for a fight."

"You and I both know how the other communicates, we've been together way too long to try to lie to one another. I mean, we *were* together." He cleared his throat, wishing he hadn't made the stupid misstep. "Something is wrong, and when there was something wrong, you always took it out on me. You made me jump through hoops in an attempt to break down your walls before you could just open up and tell me what it was that was bothering you in the first place. We've played this game a thousand times."

"Are you implying that I'm trying to manipulate you?" she countered.

He had to hold back the urge to roll his eyes. "That's not what I'm saying at all. I think you have just learned a way, albeit an unhealthy one, to get a man—me—to get you to open up. You obviously had to get to this point for a reason. Maybe it was my fault, or maybe it was something left over from something else in your life. All I'm saying is that I wish we could just openly talk to each other without fighting. It would save time and a whole hell of a lot of unnecessarily hurt feelings."

Her jaw clenched even tighter.

Sometimes he really needed to learn when to shut the hell up. "Don't be offended. That's not what I'm going for here, I just…"

What in the hell am I trying to say? Damn it. This was going so wrong.

"I just want to help you," he sighed.

"Mmm-hmm," she grumbled.

Say something. Give me a clue that I'm forgiven. That I wasn't wrong in saying what needed to be said, even if it sucked. It sucked for both of us. Tell me there is hope…hope for a friendship. I—no, we—need each other more than ever.

She pulled her car to a stop in front of an apartment complex. It was three floors, and people were coming and going around them. As he moved to unbuckle, she stopped him with the touch of her hand to his chest. "Wait." She stared out the window to her left. "Damn it."

"What? What's wrong?"

"Er," she said, biting her cheek, "my ex is here."

"*Here?* As in the parking lot? In the building? In your apartment? Explain." His fingers twitched toward the Glock always tucked into his waistband.

"Whoa there, Quick Draw McGraw, I said it was my ex, not the lead terrorist on an international watch list." She sent him a sexy half smile, one that had the power to make him almost forget his damned name.

Ex, terrorist, what difference was there when it came to people screwing with his personal life? He should have assumed she'd dated, but somehow, especially after learning about Joe, he'd figured she'd been alone. That was crazy, though. She was a beautiful, smart woman. Even if she'd not been interested in being a fish in the dating sea, some eager man would have tried to reel her in.

He had so many questions about the man, but he barely knew where or how to start asking about everything he wanted to know. So he went with the most obvious. "Are you guys still seeing one another? You know, late-night hookups or whatever?"

"No." She laughed, the sound high and scoffing. "Besides, would you really want to know?"

So he was yet to be forgiven for his saying the truth. Some things between them would never change. As it was, there was no chance they were ever going to be anything other than two single parents working to raise one single child.

How had his life gotten so screwed up in just a matter of hours?

"His name is Ben." She paused, waiting to be barraged by questions.

Mike remained silent out of fear that whatever he said would later be used against him in the Summer Daniels court. He had never liked a single dude named Ben, and apparently that trend wasn't going to come to an end anytime soon.

"He says he's an engineer for a petroleum company out of the North Dakota oil fields."

So, this Ben was rich, probably hot, and probably a total ass.

Then again, what should it have mattered to him? So what if she had moved on and started dating again? Just because Mike hadn't, it didn't mean that she would follow the same trajectory. Besides, it wasn't like they would be getting back together. He and Summer could barely have a civil conversation, let alone attempt to build a future together.

"If you guys aren't still hooking up, why would your ex be here unannounced?"

She chewed at the inside of her cheek. "He isn't exactly a nice guy. I thought he was great at first, he was so helpful and kind about Joe, and then... I don't know. Something shifted and he became this possessive man-demon. I made him leave."

"Is he harassing you?"

She sighed. "I wouldn't call it harassment exactly. He is definitely not taking the breakup well, and he doesn't want to let things go between us, but he usually respects my boundaries. And then sometimes he just shows up like this. Usually, he is making some kind of grand gesture in hopes that I will take him back."

"Then that is not him respecting your boundaries. If anything, it's him pressing against them and hoping you will relent, loosen up what lines you've drawn with him. He is trying to wear you down."

She rolled her eyes, the motion somewhat juvenile and in direct contrast to the woman he knew. That meant one thing: she knew he was right and didn't want to admit it aloud in front of him. Of course she was smart enough to know exactly what was happening in her personal life, even if she didn't want to face the truth.

"No matter what Ben thinks, he is not going to be allowed back into my life. At least, not in any kind of meaningful way." She paused. "And you're wrong. I don't think he wants me back, well, at least not *just* me. I think he liked the little family unit we had going for a while. He loved Joe and the patriarchal role he got to have in our lives."

Though Mike knew it wasn't her intention to stab him square in his heart, her words still landed a blow. Here was a man, Ben, who was fighting to have what Mike himself should have been fighting for…what he *was* trying to fight for.

But which battle was harder—the one to garner a place in Joe's and Summer's lives, or the one in his heart?

All he wanted to do right now was to get Ben out

of the picture. If that meant him charging over to Ben's car and giving him a piece of his mind, and likely a quick kick to the ass, so be it. As long as it meant he was out of his way. There were a lot of battles he could fight, some of which he could win, but he didn't think he could also take on this fight and come out of this looking like a superhero.

He'd have to be careful. He didn't want to step on Summer's toes, but at the same time he wanted her to know he would do whatever it took to make her happy.

"If you want, I'd be more than willing to have a chat with him. I could make it clear to him that you no longer want him showing up at your place."

She sent him a look that made Mike question the validity of his offer. Maybe he'd already overstepped his bounds when it came to the other dude. He was never going to get anything right when it came to Summer.

"I appreciate the offer, but in case you forgot, I have never been one of those women who want others to fight their battles for them." She put her hand down on the door handle, readying to step out.

He raised his hands in surrender. "I…just… Fine. Whatever."

This whole thing? It was going to be impossible.

There was a knock on the trunk of her car and, looking back, Mike saw that there was a tall, Mack-truck-size guy staring daggers at him.

If this was her ex, it was no wonder she hadn't wanted him to go have a talk. Mike wasn't a small man by any means; he had even prided himself on being thick with muscle…not bodybuilder thick, but still stacked. And yet, if this thing came to blows, not even Mike was sure that he would win. This dude must have been the kind who lifted at least twice a day, seven days a week.

Yep. He had been right. The guy was an ass.

Or maybe, if Mike was being completely honest with himself, maybe there was a dash of inadequacy peppered through his psyche.

The man walked up to Summer's side of the car. She opened the door in a hurry and jumped out, slamming the door behind her. Maybe she was afraid Mike would lose the fight too.

The guy kept moving, so Summer couldn't block him from seeing him, calculated actions that indicated the dude wasn't as stupid as Mike had initially assumed. Though he probably couldn't take him at fists, he did have enough street skills to bring the man to his knees.

Though Summer had closed the car door behind her, Mike tried not to listen to their conversation, though it was barely muffled through the thin glass of the car's windows. He turned around and faced the back of the car seat where Joe was sucking away on a pacifier.

"Hi, little guy," he said, smiling at him in the mirror attached to the headrest of the back seat.

Joe smiled up at him, the pacifier teetering at the edge of his mouth.

"We are going to play football when you get bigger. Would you like that?" he asked, his voice high and pleasing.

Joe gurgled in response. The sound made him chuckle. But as the noise escaped him, Summer yelled, "No! That is crap. You have no business. How dare you!"

The teetering blue pacifier dropped from Joe's lips and, at the sound of his mother's angry voice, tears started to well in the baby's eyes. His lip quivered. A piercing wail filled the air.

Mike unbuckled his seat belt, turned fully around and unstrapped the baby. "It's okay, little guy. They are just doing adult stuff. I don't like it, either," he cooed, trying to comfort his son.

If this was how Summer and her ex communicated with one another, it was no wonder they hadn't lasted. Though she and Mike had had their fair share of problems when they had been together, they had never fought like that. They had both respected each other enough not to let their disagreements turn into screaming matches.

He scooped Joe into his arms and started to gently rock back and forth with him as he hummed "Two Little Blackbirds." Joe's cries started to subside, but he still whimpered as his mother and Ben stood outside the car and yelled.

Mike'd never seen Summer like that before, that angry or that loud. Even when she had been royally pissed with him, she had stormed away. Had she changed since they had broken up? Had he turned her into this raging woman?

Ben called Summer a word that didn't bear repeating.

That was it. That was the final straw.

He stepped out of the car, Joe perched on his hip as he walked around to the driver's side. "Look, I know there is something going on here, and frankly I don't care. But what I do care about is that you are having a screaming match out in the middle of the parking lot in front of your neighbors and my son. If you guys can't control yourselves, then you need to go inside or put a pin in this until you both come to your senses and decide to act like adults."

Ben stared daggers at him. "And who the hell do you think you are that you think you can come out here and talk to me like this?"

Mike handed Joe off to Summer. "First of all, I'm Joe's father. The name's Mike. And, second of all, if you are looking for a fight, I'm more than happy to oblige. At least you would be picking one with someone who stands a chance. Or do you just face off with women?"

Ben moved his head side to side as though popping his neck in preparation for a rumble.

Oh yeah, Mike was definitely going to get his butt kicked, but if it meant taking the pressure off of Summer, at least it was for a good reason.

"Look, Ben, I've heard all about you and what a crappy dude you were to Summer. So, I don't know how you think you can stand there and talk to me like you have some kind of moral high ground. You are the lowest piece of garbage—"

Summer stepped between them. "Stop. You two need to stop."

Two apartments down, a man opened his front door and stepped outside.

They were definitely drawing all kinds of the wrong attention.

"Look, let's go to my place. We can all talk and—"

"There is no way that I'm going to walk into an apartment with this jerk," Ben said, thrusting his thumb in Mike's direction.

Yeah, he certainly felt like a jerk right now for stepping into the middle of Summer's personal relationship, but then again, he wasn't the one using expletives to talk about Summer. The man didn't have any kind of room to judge him; at least he knew how to treat women.

"Yeah, you're right, Ben, if we both walk into that apartment, only one of us will walk out."

Ben laughed, the sound low and dangerous. "I know you think you are some kind of badass, that you kill people for a living and get away with it. But I've got your number. I know exactly who you are and what you are actually capable of."

Summer talking about Mike to anyone, especially another one of her lovers, felt like a huge slap in his face. He had always thought that, given the nature of his work and the promises they had made to one another, she would never divulge any of the information that he had shared with her about him or what he did. He was supposed to be nothing more than a shadow in her life, a faceless someone from her past—as far as other men were concerned. And yet it seemed as though she had compromised his safety. But that was a fight he was going to have to shelve for now.

Mike smiled, matching Ben's malice. "That's good. Then I don't need to tell you how serious I am, and how much I mean that if I ever see you again, or if you are ever around my son or Summer, I will hunt you down."

"I sure as hell know you don't know who I am, but I hope to hell you do know the woman you are trying to stick up for." Ben looked over at her and smirked. "She isn't the pristine little angel she pretends to be. She might as well be called Black Widow with as many men as she has killed when they walked out of her bed… It's a wonder you and I are even still alive."

Summer pulled a gun from behind her waistband and pointed it square at Ben's center mass. "Get the hell out of here, Ben, or you will be the next one I kill."

Chapter Six

Summer had not anticipated things going as they had, or she would have just kept on driving until they were back in Missoula. Now, she had a whole hell of a lot of explaining to do.

They watched as Ben got into his car and squealed his tires as he pulled out of the apartment complex's parking lot.

She couldn't blame him for being pissed off with her; she hadn't wanted to get into a yelling match, either. That was always the last tool in her arsenal... well, that and her Glock. She slipped the subcompact back into the holster nestled into the crook of her stomach just over her appendix.

"Please tell me that was the one and only time you have ever pulled a gun on someone you didn't intend on shooting." Mike took Joe back from her, like her pulling a gun on the man who had threatened to do her harm in some way made her a delinquent parent.

"If he didn't leave, who said I wasn't going to shoot him? You don't know what Ben is capable of."

"No, but he seemed to know exactly what you are

capable of…and *me* for that matter." Mike hesitated, but she had already heard the hurt in his voice. "How does he know about me? About my past? Does he know who I work for? What I do?"

She stared at her feet. "I never told Ben what you did. He just sort of figured it out over time. He doesn't know who you work for or what you do…at least not really. He just assumed."

"And you didn't bother to tell him not to assume certain things?" Mike countered. "You know that his knowing severely compromises me. Who in the hell else knows who I am and what I do?" As he spoke, his words came faster and faster as the rage burned through him. "And now he knows what I look like, he could pick me out of a lineup. Do you want him… do you want *me*…to end up dead?"

"You know I would never intentionally put you in danger, ever. Your secrets have always been and will always be safe with me. I didn't tell him anything. He just wanted to get a rise out of you. Please. Mike, believe me." Her chest clenched as she thought about the times she should have stopped Ben from ever even broaching the subject about her exes. Yet, Ben had always been adamant in comparing himself to all the others she had once had in her life.

Keeping him at arm's length while she had been investigating him and his job at Rockwood had forced her to make far too many compromises when it came to her own well-being. Being a spy and infiltrating the Rockwood network to find out who had been stealing secrets had been more of a challenge than she could have ever expected. It was why she had broken things off with Ben and then requested more training before she was thrown too deeply back into the Rockwood—or any—clandestine investigation.

It was hard to believe her past, present and future were all colliding into this one epic mess.

She didn't know what to say or to do to make things right; avoidance seemed like her only option. So she smiled, the action forced, but it was the only appeasement she knew would work in a moment like this. "You want to come in and see my place? It's not much, but it is mine." There was a touch of sultry familiarity in her voice.

Mike sighed, as though he knew exactly what she was doing to get him to ignore the awkwardness between them.

Without waiting for him to speak, she walked to her door and let them in. As he made his way into her box-filled den with its one leather recliner and a baby swing, she was overcome with embarrassment. This place was a far cry from her Barbie dream house, but after the breakup it was all she could find. Great Falls had some nice apartments, but mostly they had military families and officers from nearby Malmstrom Air Force Base as their long-term tenants.

Mike put Joe down and he sat upright for a moment, then he broke in to a mad-dash crawl toward a stuffed octopus near the swing.

"Dang. That kid is fast," Mike said with a laugh.

He could pretend not to notice the stains on the

carpet and the dog scratches at the corner of the entryway all he wanted, but she knew what he had to be thinking.

"I don't plan on being here for long. I just need to figure things out at work and then we will get a real place. Ya know?"

"You don't need to worry about what I think about your place. I told you, I get it."

"Do you want something to drink?" she asked, pointing to the only chair in the place. "I'll go get you something. I think I have some…" She did a quick inventory of what she could possibly have in her fridge. If she remembered correctly, there may have been a beer, but only one.

"Water is fine." He looked toward her kitchen and had to have been noticing that the only thing on the counters was a bargain-basement toaster.

It was a harsh reality to see a person's makeshift life through the eyes of another. "You can tell I've become a bit of a minimalist." She laughed nervously as she walked to the kitchen, grabbed a glass and filled it from the tap.

"How long have you been living here?" Mike asked, sitting next to Joe on the floor and picking up the octopus. He tapped Joe's nose with one of the octopus's tentacles, making Joe gurgle and smile.

"Just a few months." Well, if a *few* meant about six.

"How long did you and Ben date after we broke up?"

She didn't know that exact date, either. Ever since the wedding had been called off and she had given birth to Joe, everything had been a whirl of well-baby checkups and trips to the store for baby supplies added into the jumble of trying to get her career moving in the right direction. Ben had been a stepping stone for her career, but she could hardly tell that to Mike.

"I don't know how long we were together, to be honest. I mean we were friends, then stayed together a lot, and he was great with Joe for the most part…"

"Does he really work for a petroleum company?" Mike prodded, the question coming from out of nowhere.

She gave him a befuddled look as her body clenched. "Why do you ask?"

"Don't you think it a bit odd that your boyfriend was working out of North Dakota, but living dozens of hours away in a nowhere town at the edge of a military base best known for nuclear weapons?"

She had contemplated Ben's inane cover story more times than she had wanted to, but it was how he had always asked her to introduce him. "What about it? You know just as well as I do that most people can telecommute now."

"I agree. But you can't tell me that he moved to Great Falls because of the beauty of the place."

Great Falls was as nasty as Medusa's stare in the winter and hot, dry and unforgiving in the summer. It was flat and desolate, and the winds ripped through the plains all year 'round, but there was an austere, understated beauty to the place. It definitely wasn't a tropical paradise that drew in nature lovers, though.

Problem number two with Ben's story. But it had been *his* story.

"You and I both know that, given the nature of our jobs, we tend to respect secrets." She wanted to tell him the truth, tell him who Ben really was, but now wasn't the time. It would only make this fight worse and threaten their safety.

"And yet you told him what I did."

So, he wasn't going to let it go. Odd that her palace didn't make him so gobsmacked that he forgot about their fight. She chuckled, the sound admittedly out of place and wrong in the tense world that rested between them. "I already told you, I didn't tell him anything."

"Have you lost your damned mind?"

Oh no, you don't. Her hackles rose as his inflammatory accusation drifted down like a spent ember.

"Excuse me?" she challenged, letting his words flitter through his psyche so he could hear exactly how wrong they were before she chose to answer.

"I…" he started then said, "I didn't mean it like that. I just mean, I am surprised that you would let a man like Ben, one whose story doesn't quite fit, this close to Joe. You have always been the kind to ask too many questions, to make sure that everything lines up and is triple-checked. What happened?"

Again, did he really want to ask her that question? It seemed like he was asking her to rain fury down. And yet his words struck home. She *had* made a mistake, a huge mistake in letting Ben in their lives. But she had been doing her job, and sometimes the lines between personal and professional had to be blurred because of Joe's age and his intense needs.

"First, things between Ben and me were never what I would call serious." She took a quick breath, trying to check her anger before it flew from her lips. "You. Joe. Life. That is what happened to me. I don't know if you can tell or not," she said, motioning all around her apartment, "but I'm struggling a bit right now. I'm trying my hardest to do all the things and do them well, and when a man came into my life wanting virtually nothing but to be a source of love and kindness, I let down my guard and let him in. Can you blame me after all you put me through?"

The silence between them was broken only with the sounds of Joe talking gibberish to his toy.

"I think it's ridiculous that you think you can come in here and start judging me for the way I've conducted my life," she raged. "I had a plan. I had a man I loved in my life. I had my world figured out and I was preparing to run, to make this life everything I had ever dreamed of, and you pulled it all out from under my feet. You are the one who needs to answer for what life has become. Not me."

She was pretty sure she could see a red welt rising on his face where she had just slapped him with her words.

"I'm so, so sorry," Mike said, moving near enough that he could wipe a tear from the corner of her eye.

Damn it, why did she have to cry when she was angry?

She moved away from his touch, not letting him console her.

He had done this. He deserved to watch her fall apart in front of him. To bear witness to the ravaging effects of one decision…a decision she had not been able to make with him and yet that had had the power to strip her future away.

Screw him.

From the way he moved into her, she could tell that he wanted to pull her into his arms and console her. He'd always been so damned good at making her forget the pain, and yet she doubted his touch would work like it once had. After a person crushed a soul, they no longer held the power or tools to rebuild it.

She was the only one who could rebuild her life. And right now, that meant boxes where there should have been chairs and questions where there should have been answers. Mike was just going to have to deal with what she had done with her life, whether he liked it or not.

"I never thought—"

"Yeah, that's one of the truest statements you've ever made," she said, her words laced with venom.

His shoulders fell and he looked crestfallen. "You're right. I didn't think. I would have never asked you to marry me, I would have never dated you, if this is what I thought would happen. I have only ever wanted what was best for you."

Though she was fuming with anger, she believed him. Mike wasn't a bad man. There was no way that he could have ever wanted to hurt her as he had, but that didn't make the pain any less real. It only meant that he was as clumsy and as ill suited to love as she was.

"You weren't the only person in the relationship. I chose you and wanted the best too."

And though this was a low point, she couldn't say she actually regretted falling in love with Mike. He had given her a beautiful baby boy and many hours of happy and blissful memories. And, oh, the way he had once been able to make her laugh.

"You were proof to me that I could really love," Mike said, sending her a soft look that made all the anger still pulsing through her seep through the tips of her toes and disappear into the ground.

It was that look and his unexpected moments of sweetness that had made her fall in love with him in the first place. He had so many facets to him and, standing here, looking at him, she was reminded of what a great man he was…and how much she missed having him in her life. And yet she couldn't let herself be swept up by him again. As sweet as Mike could be, he could become equally cold and hard.

He moved in closer to her, so close she could feel his breath against the skin of her face. Her heart thrashed in her chest, just as confused by all the emotions it was feeling as she was. The ancient Egyptians had believed the center of all thought was the heart; and in this moment, she could understand how an entire culture could believe such a thing. Her heart definitely had a mind of its own, one totally independent of the logical and rational thoughts that filled her brain.

He didn't love her and she didn't love him. At least, not like that, not like this moment, this closeness, seemed to indicate. Sure, she would love him as the father of her son and the man she had once promised her life to, but now it couldn't be that way. They could only love one another for the people they had become, people who were strangers to one another. He only knew her before the pain.

And yet, when he leaned in close and his lips brushed against hers, she didn't back away. The kiss started slow, gentle as a butterfly's wings' caress against her skin. Perhaps he was just as afraid of what was about to happen as she was, but yearning for her as she was for him.

Yearning. That was it. This wasn't love. This wasn't something so stupid. This was just her body needing his body. Nothing more. It was the familiar. *He* was the familiar.

She wrapped her arms around his neck and ran her fingers through the back of his shaggy hair. It was odd how, in a moment like this, she was reminded of how much she had loved his soft hair and the way it felt in her fingers while his lips pressed against hers. It was the conglomeration of sensations—the soft and the firm, the hot and the cold, and the push and the pull—that had always made this man so... So right.

She moaned into his mouth as his hungry kiss grew more voracious. He felt so good pressed against her, his body telling hers that he had missed her just as much as she had missed him.

Maybe they weren't really strangers, after all.

Maybe his leaving her had just been a stupid mistake.

She had made mistakes.

She could forgive him.

Yes.

Especially if he kept kissing her. His lips moved down her neck and his hand moved up beneath her shirt, finding its way under the cloth of her bra. He thumbed her nipple, making it harden and ache for the warm softness of his mouth.

And then Joe laughed, the sound bright and cheery.

The sound stopped the advance.

Mike pulled back and Summer readjusted her shirt, suddenly feeling like a teenager who had just been caught making out by a wayward parent.

Running her hand over her hair, it came to rest on her neck in the place where Mike had just been kissing her. Oh, and had he been kissing her.

Mike did a little sidestep and turned away from her to face Joe. He scooped him up in his arms and lifted him toward the ceiling, laughing as he moved. "You! You know how to ruin a moment, don't you?" He laughed. "You are definitely my kiddo, Mr. Man."

Joe giggled, arching his back like he was doing a baby version of Superman as Mike walked him around up in the air. "'It's a bird. It's a plane…'"

"It's mother nature's best form of birth control," she finished, laughing.

Mike lowered Joe onto his hip. He came over and gave her a long, soft kiss on the cheek. "Maybe we should have had a kid together a long time ago."

His words came as a surprise. So much so, she didn't know what to say.

Just yesterday she had thought that Mike was going to be furious with her, that he was never going to speak to her again after she told him about Joe. And now, here they were almost falling into the trap of being a happy family.

This…this was far too good to last. She had to tell him the truth before things went any further and she hurt him. If she told him now, he might still forgive her.

"Mike, I have to tell you something."

The joy that filled his face drifted away as he must have recognized the reserve in her tone. "What?"

"Promise me that you won't be angry with me if I tell you," she countered.

He frowned. "That is like asking someone to forgive you for a mistake you know you are about to make, and yet you don't stop."

Oh, this was going to be a mistake, no doubt. But some things had to be said, some truths had to be known. Without them, there were only false starts and empty promises.

If he was going to come back into their lives, he needed to come back fully aware of what that would mean for them all.

"You know I worked for STRIKE…" She paused. "Yeah."

She hadn't meant that as a question, but she was glad for the moment to collect her thoughts. "Well, things go a little deeper than that." She looked down at her hands.

But did she really need to feel as sullen as she did? She'd not known this would be where things would head with them; if anything, she had just been looking for the right moment to really open up to him and tell him the truth. She needed to know, regardless of their past, that she could still trust him.

And though she wasn't entirely sure she could, she had to try. She had to tell him the truth about Ben, and what he had come here for, and then let the chips fall.

She wanted Mike to say something, but he just stood there looking at her, studying her and waiting for her. The silence was more painful than she could have expected.

"You were right about Ben. He doesn't just work for a petroleum company—it's a little more complicated than that."

He scoffed, stepping back from her. "No crap. I called that."

She chewed at her bottom lip, wishing she had allowed the kiss to keep going instead of standing there and exposing her weak points.

"He wasn't here to get back together, was he?" Mike continued.

She shook her head.

"What *did* he want from you?"

She swallowed back the fear that had pooled in

her throat. "He and I...we both worked for the same team at a certain point. We don't anymore. And when I quit, apparently they came to suspect some things about me, thanks to Ben. Things I can't tell you about. But if they find out that there is any validity to the rumors, they are going to take Joe and kill me. Mike, I'm afraid."

Mike's eyes widened and she was sure she saw flames at their centers. "And here I thought I needed to be a gentleman. If I ever see Ben again, he's as good as dead."

Chapter Seven

Mike wanted to go back in time and take Ben out. One little tap of the trigger and Summer's problem would be handled for good. He really should have trusted his gut about the guy, but it was hard to look at any situation objectively when it involved an ex and their newest fling.

He just couldn't get over the fact that Summer had let this man into her life. Seeing Ben as merely a jerk of an ex, a man who didn't know how to treat women, was bad enough, but then add a death threat and it took his hate toward the guy impossibly deeper.

Ben had to go.

"I'll take care of him. Where does he live? He can't be that far ahead of me. I bet I can still get the drop on him." Mike's thoughts were a flurry of whats, buts and whys. He needed to be logical. Stop his mouth and click on his brain. But first he needed some answers. "Does he think you will tell me who he is? The threat I pose to him?"

If the guy was smart, he would already be heading for the hills in anticipation that Mike would be just about to come bearing down on him. No matter the status of Mike and Summer's relationship, she was the mother of his son and if anyone dared threaten them, hell would have no greater fury.

The man had to know his ass was on the line. That meant any sort of element of surprise was well out of the question.

If only he had taken the lead when he had first heard about this dude, maybe it wouldn't have played out like this. Mike could have lied about who he was, what he was doing there…if only Summer had told him the truth earlier. If only she had been honest about her ex with him well before their confrontation.

Summer opened her mouth, about to answer, but Mike waved her off. "Never mind. I answered my own damned question."

He paced around the apartment, thinking about the resources he had on hand and what he could quickly access if he was in a pinch. STEALTH had operatives all around the world and if he needed… No, this was a personal matter. He didn't want to bring in his siblings or any other members of the team to handle this. He could kill the bastard himself.

"Wait. Ben isn't the bad guy here," Summer said, raising her hands in surrender. "I mean he isn't a good guy, but *he* isn't the one threatening my life—he was only the messenger. Don't get ahead of yourself."

The anger seeped from his pores, but instead of diminishing, it changed direction. "What in the hell are you talking about? I thought you just said that he came here and threatened you and Joe, that you were in danger."

"Yes, but it's the entire group I'm worried about. Even if we take Ben out, they could be coming for me."

He was so confused. What all had she gotten herself into? And how had she fallen prey to this group who threatened her life?

"You need to explain to me what the hell is going on. If not, I can't... I'll take care of Joe, but..."

She looked at him like he had just asked her to tell him the location of the last unicorn so he could go and murder it.

"I know this is uncomfortable. I know you don't want to tell me. And I'm not going to judge you for whatever the hell happened to wrap you up in this mess. But I need to know what I'm going to face. We need to be prepared in order to keep you and Joe safe."

She chewed on her lip. "If I tell you the truth, you have to promise that you won't tell anyone... Ever. And you can't judge me for this. I... I have been struggling."

He nodded, but fear rattled through him. What had he done to her that she'd felt compelled to get involved with Rockwood—and maybe worse—to provide for herself and her son? If only he had followed through on their wedding, none of this would have ever happened. Instead, they could have been living in a house of their own, maybe something along the river like they had always dreamed about, and he could be playing out in the yard with Joe. Instead, here they were, needing to run for their lives, and it was all his fault.

He had tried to do the right thing, and it had come back to bite not only him but all of them square in the ass.

"I have no room to judge," he said, trying to not self-flagellate when he'd have years to think about all the things he had done wrong. "I'm here to listen and help, nothing more." It felt strange saying that, but he absolutely meant it.

"After our breakup, STRIKE and I had a bit of a falling out. They weren't using me much, I'm sure it was because I was a massive train wreck." She sucked in a long breath and, as she paused, he could almost hear what she was going to tell him next. "Another company approached me, asked if I would like to be involved with their cyber team working on government-issued contracts. They had me working undercover."

He chomped on his lip, trying to stop himself from saying anything that would upset her and stall her confession.

She looked away, guilty. "I was doing really well as a double agent, and after Solomon Scot—Kate's father—was killed, the group I was working for with Ben had me doing industrial espionage, spying on ConFlux, trying to get military engineering secrets. I got them and handed them off to Ben. Before Ben and his colleagues could use them, the codes were changed, access denied. I came out okay, and Con-Flux didn't lose anything."

"Were you gathering and selling state secrets, Summer?" He took his phone out of his pocket, thinking about Zoey. Maybe she could help them, maybe she knew someone in the higher-ups who could pull some strings and get Summer out of this jam. Treason was serious business.

But he put his phone down on a nearby box. No. If he told Zoey, she would want to know everything. She would ask far too many questions he didn't know the answers to. He had to play this smart. *They* had to.

"It appeared like I was—at least to the people whose group I was infiltrating. But all I knew at the time was that I was to find a way into the ConFlux network, grab a specific set of codes for my main team, and then leave the door open for the rest of the teams. Kate was in on it. She knew that we were trying to bait a trap and pull out anyone who was trying to steal American military secrets."

Mike didn't know what to think about all of this. There was so much information, so many secrets and so many twists. Summer had gotten herself much deeper into the world of spies and counterspies than he could have imagined.

"It was then, when I met up with Kate, that Ben might have seen me. Maybe he connected the dots, or someone did… I think I may have compromised my work."

"This is crazy," he grumbled. "You. Me. This is crap. You were *stealing* military-grade secrets."

She raised her hands in supplication. "That's not it… I was just doing my job. I am working for and loyal to the good guys. I swear."

Mike opened his mouth. She hadn't told him enough so that he could really believe her, and he wasn't sure that he wanted her to bring him any deeper into her blurry-lined world than she already had. She was a spy. What if she was using him to spy on STEALTH? She had been asking questions about Rockwood, too.

He struggled to connect the dots based on everything she had told him so far.

Joe crawled toward the couch, and after bonking his head on the corner of a box, he started to cry. Mike swooped in and picked him up just as Summer moved to get him. "He'll be okay," she said, her tone soft and cooing as she gently cupped her son's head and nodded. "He's a tough boy. Aren't you, baby?"

Joe rubbed his eyes as he sniffled and then took hold of Summer's finger.

The simple action threatened to rip out Mike's heart and trample it on the ground. This was his family; he had unintentionally made this family and, as angry and upset as he was, he would do whatever it took to make sure they were all safe.

He rocked him, trying to comfort his son. As he swayed side to side, it occurred to Mike that this little man in his arms was perhaps a sponge for all the emotions swirling around him. If that was the case, even though he didn't understand the conversation, it was still doing the child no good.

Joe stuck his thumb in his mouth and looked up at him, his blinks starting to get slower and slower.

"Do you have somewhere we can put him down for a little nap? I think our boy is getting sleepy," he said.

"As soon as you put him down in the crib, he will wake right up. He hates being alone. But you're right, our little guy looks sleepy. Most of the time, when he fights it, I take him for a little drive in the car." Summer looked toward the window. "We left his seat out there in the car. We can take him for a short ride. You know, drive around a bit until he's fast asleep."

The last thing he wanted to do was to put the kiddo down and upset him.

He chuckled as he realized what he had been thinking. Here he had only known he was a dad for a day and yet this little being already had him wrapped around the tiniest of his fingers. It was only too easy to fall so desperately in love with a child.

It was strange, but once upon a time, he had fallen in love with Summer almost as quickly.

"I'm going to freshen up and grab some things for his diaper bag. I will meet you out there in a few minutes," she said.

"I'll go put him in the car seat. Sound good?"

"Great." She headed toward the back bedrooms. "The car's unlocked, but the keys are beside the door." She motioned to the peg where her keys were hanging.

He looked down at Joe, who was sucking away on his thumb, still fighting the sandman. "It's okay, little man, you can give up the ghost. Papa has you, you're safe."

As she disappeared down the hall, Mike made his way outside. Ben was nowhere to be seen and the apartment complex had slipped into the midday sleepiness that came when it was a warm late-fall day. It was cooler outside than it had been in the apartment. No wonder Joe liked sleeping in the air-conditioned car far more than sitting in the muggy crib.

Truth be told, Mike could have gone for a nap too. His mind wandered to Kate and Summer working together. Had Summer told Kate about Joe? Had Kate told his brother? Did people in his family know that he had a child and yet no one had told him?

He was furious, but he was also so freaking confused. Could he be mad at his teams for keeping a secret from him when they were all members of a shadow team? Everything they did was for a reason. No doubt, no one wanted to be the person to tell him about a son he didn't know he'd had when that was Summer's decision to make.

And who knew, maybe Summer hadn't told them about Joe. She hadn't given any clues outwardly that she had a kid when he had first seen her. It was more than plausible she hadn't wanted to put any of his family or team in such a compromising position by telling Kate about the baby.

She hadn't wanted to leave the news on his voice

mail, so there was no way she would put the power of this revelation in the hands of anyone else.

He opened the back door of the car and put Joe into his car seat. As he pulled the straps over Joe's arms, the thumb went right back into his mouth and he turned his head to the side as though the little guy knew exactly what was going to happen next and he was just readying himself to fall asleep.

Mike couldn't be angry. Not really. Not when he had been given such a tremendous gift. Summer had tried to talk to him. He hadn't listened. By her stepping forward at the wedding, she had granted him access to their baby. She hadn't had to do what she had done. There had been other options.

He couldn't even imagine how it would have felt only to learn in twenty years that he'd had a child, after Joe was grown and likely starting to think about having a family of his own. She could have held out. She could have been so angry with him that she could have denied him the opportunity to be involved in their child's infancy. And yet she had forgiven him enough to let him in.

She had mucked up her life and she had gotten herself into trouble, but if they worked together, this potential compromising position was something they could get her out of. It would be hard, sure, but maybe with a few of the right phone calls to the right people, she could be safe.

But that didn't mean he didn't need some answers both from her and from his team.

He reached down and moved to pull his phone

from his pocket, but realized he'd left it sitting on top of the box in the living room. And, he'd left the keys hanging beside the door. He needed to run back inside.

Joe had his eyes closed and his head was resting comfortably on the gray polka dots of the car seat's lining. Mike glanced around, looking for a button or something that would unlatch the car seat from its base, but there were a million little red buttons and tabs and he wasn't sure which was the self-destruct button. Joe looked so at ease that Mike didn't want to go through the motions of trying to unbuckle him.

There was no one around, no cars coming or going, and he would only be inside for a second... But every part of his being told him not to leave the child alone. He looked down at Joe, whose eyes were now closed. His head dipped in sleep but jerked back up, eyes still closed.

His son was definitely a fighter. Hopefully he would remain that way for the rest of his life—it was the only way to come out the other side of it in a way that was true to a person's soul.

How had Summer been able to be a single parent? This was such a simple thing and yet, by himself, it was immeasurably hard. He couldn't imagine going through these seemingly easy, inconsequential moments where a person was stuck between a rock and hard place. She really was deserving of some kind of an award.

He wouldn't let her be on her own with his kiddo ever again. Joe needed a father and Summer needed a teammate, someone she could call whenever she needed anything.

He held his breath as he pushed the red button near the top of the car seat and it unlatched from the base. Thankfully, Joe didn't stir.

He walked to the apartment and set the car seat down just inside the door. He pushed the door gently, barely closing it behind him as he made his way into the living room to grab his phone.

Dude, seriously, this was rough. This back-and-forth thing. How did a parent get anything done?

He'd heard many new parents complain about the inability to even do something as simple as take a shower when they had a new baby, and now he finally understood it. It wasn't that they were incapable of showering, it was the anxiety that kept them needing to see where their child was and what they were doing at every second of every day.

He suddenly felt sorry for his own parents. The hell he and his siblings must have put them through. At what point had they started to loosen the reins on their kids and started trusting that they would be safe? Or did they ever really assume they were safe? What if this fear never went away? He doubted that it did. Rather, it had likely only been dampened by the ravages of time and the need to keep moving forward and through the crippling anxiety.

How did parents live like this, regardless of the age of their children?

He grabbed his phone and glanced down the L-shaped hallway in the direction of what he assumed was Summer's bedroom. "I don't know how you do it," he yelled toward her.

"What?" she asked, her voice muffled behind the door.

"I said, I don't know how you do it."

"Huh?"

He walked down the hall and to the left until he was standing outside the closed door. "I said, I don't know how you do it."

"Do what?" she asked, moving closer to the other side of the door.

"This. Be a single parent. It seems like it's a real juggling act."

She gave a sarcastic laugh. "You don't even know. You've only been at this for a day. And, honestly, I don't know how I'm doing it. I have to admit that I feel like I'm literally figuring this out minute by minute."

That, he totally understood.

He rested his forehead on the door for a moment. "Thank you, Summer."

"Huh? For what?"

He put his hand on the white paint of the paneled door, it was cool under his fingertips. "For letting me into your guys' life. I know things must have been so hard for you. But you don't have to go through any of this by yourself anymore. I'm here for you. I don't expect that we will always see eye to eye, and we will probably fight about a lot of things, but whenever you need anything you know I have your and Joe's back."

There was a long silence from inside the room. "Thanks, Mike. And hey, you know I'm sorry."

"What do you have to be sorry about?" He had been the one to put all this chaos into motion.

"I'm sorry for not telling you sooner. I hope you know I tried."

"I know... I know you tried." He paused, still angry with himself. "I am the one who needs to be sorry. I *am* sorry."

He could hear her breathing right on the other side of the door, like she was standing parallel to him, sharing this moment of pain. He wanted to open the door and pull her into his arms, but if he was touching her or even just seeing her, he wasn't sure that he had the power it would take to say all the things he needed to say.

"I think we need to go to the feds with all this."

There was a long pause. "No, not yet." Her voice was high, the sound false. She was still not telling him something. He could hear the hesitation and the lies in her tone.

"What company was it that you were working for—the one that is threatening you?" he asked, questioning his judgment in asking. If she told him, he might come under fire, as well. But if she didn't, he wouldn't know exactly who he was fighting.

Her breathing quickened. "Er, Ben and I...were working for a company."

"What company?" he asked, not understanding.

"Rockwood—the group that tried to have you and your brother gunned down." She paused as if to let her words sink in for a moment. In interrogation, he would have called that tactical silence. He hated it, but not as much as he hated Rockwood.

He ran his hand over his face, trying to stave off the start of a headache. "I've got to run. I left Joe alone in the hall. We can continue this conversation when you get out to the car. Hurry up."

When this woman screwed up, she screwed up royally. At least they had that one thing in common— they could both wreak havoc on their personal lives.

He hummed as he made his way back out to the hall to fetch the keys, the song just a little ditty, a reflection of the hope he was feeling even during these dark times. It was crazy, but the fact that she had been working for his enemy—or rather, had been spying on Rockwood—made him feel better. Something about this entire scenario made him feel like they were approaching even ground. Maybe this, being here with Summer and Joe, was an opportunity to put all of their lives back in order and he could be her hero and show her how much he was willing to sacrifice to be with them.

"All right, little guy, Mom is just about done. She'll be out in a minute," he said, walking toward the front door where the car seat had been sitting on the floor. However, the spot where he had put Joe was now empty and the door was ajar.

He rushed to the door, jerking it wide open and looking outside as if Joe could have gotten up and somehow moved himself. But the baby and the car seat were nowhere in sight. Someone must have been watching, reached inside the moment his back was turned and taken his son.

His heart shuddered, threatening to stop beating with the pain. Joe was gone.

Chapter Eight

His scream was something unlike anything she had ever heard before, a blood-curdling sound like a dying animal—and something that she never wanted to hear again. Summer rushed out, expecting to find Mike lying on the floor in a pool of his own blood or maybe being bludgeoned by a house bandit. Instead, he was standing beside the front door, his hand on the top of his head, staring at nothing.

"What's the matter? What happened to Joe? Is he okay?" She found herself beside him, but she had no idea how her body had gotten her there. "Where is he? Did you put him in the car?" she asked.

Not waiting for Mike to respond, she rushed outside to the car, but it sat empty.

Mike stared at the car, saying nothing for a long moment. "He's…he's gone. They must have just opened the front door and reached in. I didn't lock it. I wasn't planning on leaving him alone… I-I just…" His voice cracked as his breath seeped from his lips.

Summer couldn't hear anything over the din of terror ringing through her. Someone had taken their son. Someone had taken him. It had to have been Ben. But he had only threatened her. He hadn't said Rockwood had concrete evidence about her being a double agent. If anything, he'd just seemed pissed about the breakup. And as much as he had scared her, part of her hadn't really taken him seriously.

If Ben had wanted her dead or to kidnap Joe, why would he have done it now?

No. It didn't make sense. Ben had always come at her head-on, he wouldn't have just taken Joe and slipped away. It wasn't his way of working. He would have wanted her to see him with Joe, to witness in horror as he took him away. He would have made a show of it, making her watch what she had caused.

Besides, when they had been dating, Ben had always said he loved Joe. He had even gone so far as to talk about adopting him—not that she would have ever let that happen.

But then there were times when Ben had made it no secret that he'd thought she was a terrible mother—especially when she had gone away for days without telling him where she was going. Little had he known at the time, but she had been meeting with her boss, Kevin, at the DTRA and reporting what she had learned about Rockwood.

Maybe Ben had been pushed over the edge by seeing her with Mike. Maybe this was all some terrible and warped way for Ben to get his revenge.

Her breathing started to quicken as panic wormed through her. She pressed her forehead against the cold steel of the car door as reality hit. This was her fault.

What made it worse was that it was all because she had once again put her faith in Mike Spade. She had trusted him to watch her son. To keep him safe.

This was Mike's doing. He had left their son alone. She had told him that Rockwood was threatening to take Joe and yet he had not put her baby's safety first. Then again, Joe had been *in her apartment.* She could have made the same mistake. And yet, she had to be angry at someone other than herself.

She turned to Mike, hate filling her as she looked at his terror-stricken face. "You did this."

He didn't speak. He didn't bother to deny.

He had to have known that what she said was true—they had lost Joe because of him.

"We will get him back. *I* will get him back." Mike sounded breathless, as if the vastness of loss had stripped him of his voice.

"If you don't, I will spend the rest of my life hating you." She didn't like the words that spilled from her like blood, but she couldn't help it, she couldn't control anything anymore, least of all what she was feeling.

Her son… Her son was gone.

"I'm so sorry," he whispered. "I just put him down for a split second. I didn't think—"

"I already know that much," she seethed.

Mike ran his hands over his face and held them there, covering his eyes for a long moment as though he could strip away the reality of what he had caused. "You have every right to be upset. I screwed up. But I will get Joe back. I will set things right. I will fix this. All of this."

She opened her mouth, ready to spit more fire at him, but he stopped her when he glanced over at her. He looked like he was in physical pain, like someone had slashed through his chest and removed his heart. She knew the look because she was feeling it too.

"You can hate me all you want, but we have to work together to get Joe back. We are in this together." Mike paused. "We have to be strategic about this. We have to think. We can't let our emotions cloud our judgment. Not when Joe's life, all our lives, are on the line."

"Since when has it been *our* lives? No one is trying to gun you down." She was indignant in her pain, but she couldn't stop herself. He couldn't possibly be hurting as much as she was right now.

Mike stepped closer to her and she backed away. He couldn't fix this like he normally did, when he'd let her fall into his embrace. No. That wouldn't work anymore. Her weakness for his touch had gotten them into this mess in the first place.

"We need to call in backup. We need to get law enforcement involved. They need to know that Joe is missing."

"No." The word was a knee-jerk response, but she meant it. "Bringing them in would be a slippery slope." She stopped as she thought about all the different facets of what it would mean to bring in the locals—few of the advantages would outweigh the profusion of potential negatives. "Your team has just about the same level of resources at their disposal. Do you think they would be willing to help me out? I can pay."

"You know if this thing goes even more haywire, the police will end up getting involved. I mean what if someone gets killed? How will we come out of this looking like the good guys if we work behind the police's backs and they find out about it?"

"I hear what you are saying, but I can't expose what I've done."

"Not even if that leads to our son being returned safely?" Mike challenged.

"How dare you. That was low, even for you." She tried to control her rage. "I can't expose what I've done because it might lead to worse things happening…to Joe."

"I'm sorry," Mike huffed. "I didn't mean it like that… I mean I did, I want Joe home, but I didn't mean to attack you. I'm just as scared and upset as you are."

How could he be when he'd only just entered their lives? He didn't know the feeling of holding Joe in the hospital when he had taken his first breath. He didn't know what it was like taking care of a baby with a cold, worrying if he was going to make it through the night.

As hurt as she felt, Summer didn't voice her thoughts. He didn't deserve to be lashed with them.

He loved Joe. He loved their son just as much as she did.

Love had the power to overwhelm a person in less than a second—and she had seen it engulf Mike when he'd first held their son. Their love for their son was different, though. Hers had had more time to grow and blossom. But love, she knew, wasn't something tangible that could be measured by such feeble metrics like time. Love could only be measured by sacrifice. And here Mike was, willing to sacrifice his life for their son. No matter what she was feeling, the power of his love was undeniable.

But she wasn't ready to forgive him for everything he had put them through.

"Do you think it was Ben who took him?" Mike asked.

She shook her head, violently. "He would have made a show of it. But it very well could have been someone from Rockwood."

Mike scowled, and she could see the terror in his eyes at the possibility that just about anyone could have taken their boy.

"Did you see anyone when you came outside?" she asked, trying to shift her focus to what needed to happen next to bring Joe back.

"I didn't," he said, shaking his head. "Whoever did this had to be watching. Either they followed us or were staked out here and just waiting for an opening to get their hands on Joe."

Whichever it was, it didn't matter. They needed to assume they'd been followed and that there probably had been someone staked out and watching her. The people she was working for, or had been working for, weren't stupid, but they were dangerous and angry.

She had been part of kidnapping cases before, not on the frontlines or in the role as a negotiator, but she had seen enough of these things to know that people—and kids, specifically—were usually used to barter for ransom. She doubted Rockwood would use Joe for ransom, but why else would they have taken him instead of killing him outright? They had to have wanted something.

"They are going to reach out to us. Right now, I think all we can do is wait." She couldn't believe what she was saying. To wait went against every particle of her being as a mother, but it didn't change the reality of what was happening.

"Are you absolutely, one-hundred-percent sure that it's Rockwood behind Joe's kidnapping? You are *sure* that Ben wouldn't have done this?" Mike countered. "You know I've always said that usually the most obvious suspect is the perp."

"I know you don't like Ben, neither do I. But he loves Joe and I truly believe he wants me to be cleared of being a double agent. He wants me to come back to him. He is volatile, and he is angry, but he wouldn't compromise Joe like this. And he wouldn't compromise any possible future the three of us could have together. He loves us."

Mike nodded, but she could tell he didn't really believe her. Or maybe it was that he just didn't like what she was saying.

"Ben is a lot of things, but I really don't think he's behind this. I don't think he's the bad guy here."

Mike shook his head. "I am not trying to make Ben the bad guy. I just want to make sure that we don't waste time chasing the wrong people. But you seem to want to defend him all the time… If you still love him, that's fine. Just admit it and then we can move forward with that awareness in place."

"I don't love Ben." She could feel the truth of her words, but she wasn't sure Mike could feel them as well. "Ben was just a space filler, a soft landing, if you want to call it that. I needed someone who could staunch the loneliness in my heart after losing you, and he seemed to love me. Having him as my boyfriend made it easy to spy on Rockwood. Things with him checked a lot of the boxes for what I needed in my life." It ached to admit her folly.

"Summer…" Mike slipped his hand into hers.

There was that touch. That damned touch. He was a master of making her forget herself with that simple thing. And he would always have that power over her, no matter how much she knew she shouldn't let him.

"Let's just get Joe back, then we can think about everything else. As it stands, let's just call a truce. Fair?"

From where she stood, it was more than fair, it was a million miles past fair, given the circumstances. It was better to be a team than to fight with the one man she had always loved and always would.

Mike could never know, but it was so easy for

him to see if he wanted to—her love for him would always mean sacrifices. Sacrifices she would gladly make if it meant having him in her life.

Chapter Nine

Women made no sense at all.

He'd always hated when other men had said things like that to him, but now that he was standing there and forced to see everything that was Summer, Mike really understood it. She was just a little bit, albeit justifiably, crazy. Luckily, she was the right kind of crazy for him.

"Let's go inside. I can make some phone calls to see if we can get my team on this and then we will go from there. How does that sound?" he asked, trying to help.

She nodded. "I think we need to talk to the neighbors to see if anyone saw anything."

They could work on securing the scene all they wanted and collecting eyewitnesses, acting like this was a regular investigation that didn't personally impact them. But this was their child and they needed to fly under the radar. The second they started going around and knocking on doors, their ordeal would be out in the open, and that could trigger police involvement. Whatever anonymity they'd been hoping for would be gone.

There was a certain amount of power that came into play outside the rules and regulations of the legal system. And they would need all the leeway they could get when he got his hands on whomever had thought it acceptable to steal a baby out from under their noses. There was a certain level of hell reserved for people like that, and he would make sure they had the chance to experience the heat.

Mike shook his head. "There wasn't anyone around that I noticed. Whoever did this wouldn't have been stupid enough to be seen and, as much as I want to ask around, I doubt we'll get anything—the kidnapper seemed smart enough to watch for nosy neighbors. Plus, I think it's best if we are just quiet and lay low a little bit. Like you said, we just need to wait for the call."

As if on cue, Mike's phone pinged. The number, from Montana, was the generic type likely generated by some kind of app. He would have his team look into it, but he'd done this enough to know a spoof when he saw it.

He clicked on the message; it was simple and yet terrifying.

Baby safe. For now. You have 46 hours. Anything more and baby loses toes.

Summer gasped audibly when he showed her the text.

Yep. Someone was going to die for this. Actually, there would probably be several before he was done.

He dialed the number, wanting to hear the voice of the person responsible for the hell he was going through. A man picked up, but Mike didn't recognize the voice. "I assume you got our message and that your little girlfriend told you about what was going on and how she appears to have been playing on both sides of the fence. As it is, she is lucky to be alive."

"If you don't return Joe in the next ten minutes, it is not us who need to be worried. It will be you and your damned crew. We will hunt you down—"

"Hold it," the man said, cutting him off. "Do you think it's a good idea to threaten the person who has your girlfriend's baby?"

Damn it.

Rational. He needed to be rational.

First, he'd called Summer his "girlfriend," which meant that he was either downplaying Mike and Summer's past and using it to demoralize and deride him or that he had just been watching them for a finite period of time and had made incorrect assumptions.

Second, the guy had called Joe *her* baby and not his son, which had to mean he didn't know the truth. Together, this was good. Whoever it was didn't have all the answers, which meant he hadn't infiltrated Summer's life too deeply. He was still only at surface level, which meant Mike and Summer had some degree of autonomy and leverage.

Third, Summer had been right: the kidnapping couldn't have been perpetrated by Ben. Mike had introduced himself to Ben as Joe's father. Therefore, someone else was behind the kidnapping.

The only good news was that their enemy didn't know he could use Joe against him; as it was, he was looking at Mike like he was just a passive outsider—a mere boyfriend with little skin in the game. Well, he could play off their ill-conceived and poorly executed strategy.

"Before you make any more demands, I need to know Joe is alive and doing well. What can you do to prove that he is safe?" He forced himself into negotiation mode.

"We don't wanna hurt the baby. Our primary objective here is to get the information we need and that's it. Summer is lucky. We need the information she stole from ConFlux or she and the baby would already be dead."

"Who are you?" Mike asked, though he was more than aware these people were likely from Rockwood.

The man grunted. "Don't interrupt me again, or the baby will pay."

He shut his mouth.

"Now, your little girlfriend has come into some information. Codes…" The man paused. "If she gives us those codes, we will keep your baby alive. If she doesn't, we will make you all pay."

"Before we agree to do anything, you need to prove to me that Joe is okay." He was careful to use calculated statements, ones all about the man he was negotiating with.

The most crucial key in successful negotiation

was for the negotiator to solve the problems and to always push for additional time. But this kind of crisis response was difficult in even the best of times, times when there wasn't such a deeply personal tie. Negotiating was going to be nearly impossible if Mike kept putting things in terms of this being his own child.

"What do you want with the baby?" he asked, trying to find a baseline on their hostage taker.

"Well, the last damned thing I want is to wake his ass up to prove he is unharmed and then have to deal with a crying baby for the next few hours."

Interesting, so the guy didn't want to hurt Joe or, at least, to cause himself too much unnecessary stress. This was good.

He opened his mouth to speak, but then thought about his many hours of training. One of the first practices for negotiating in this type of circumstance was to follow the 80/20 rule. A negotiator had to keep the hostage taker talking eighty percent of the time; he should only do twenty. Next, he had to be a strong, active listener and hear the things not being said in addition to what was.

The man on the other end of the line huffed. He sounded annoyed, as if having to wait for Mike to speak and give him feedback was more than he could handle. "Look, I can send a picture of the baby. But there are conditions."

"What are the conditions?" he asked, carefully mirroring the man's language so he would feel validated.

"We want to make this as simple as possible. If you give us what we want, you can have the kid back in a matter of hours." The man halted, but Mike didn't say anything. Instead he let him continue with his demands. "We need all the codes that were taken from the ConFlux system."

"You need all the codes." Mike pushed the speaker button on his phone so Summer could listen in; the more ears he had on this, the better. Maybe she could pick up something he missed and make sense of this in a way that he was unable. "What are you planning to do with these codes?"

"That's none of your damned business, Mike."

The man had used his name. It didn't come as a huge surprise, but it was jarring, like this guy had somehow just made things a degree more personal and threatening. More, the man had used his name on purpose. Mike had clearly stumbled onto something that had caused the guy to lash out and get emotional.

"How do you think we should get these codes?" he continued, trying hard to restrain his own emotions. He couldn't backslide, they were making progress, but he needed more time and more information to safely get Joe back.

"That isn't my damned problem. My problem is that you are apparently a freaking idiot."

Okay, he needed to dial it back a bit and deescalate. "I'm not trying to be stupid, just trying to get all the facts and to fully understand your demand. This is about you, what you need."

"No, this is about the kid." The man sounded

frantic, and Mike didn't try to dissuade him. Some amount of stress on the other end of the phone was good, as long as it didn't lead to Joe's being hurt. Stress led to poor negotiation skills, which could definitely be to Mike's benefit just as long as he was careful.

Summer moved closer, as if to say something, but he stopped her with a shake of his head. She was far too angry and far too close to the situation. He pushed Mute on his phone so the man on the other end couldn't hear what he was saying.

"Summer, you need to just listen. Please. I'm going to see if we can get this guy to fold without having to play into his demand. We need Joe to be safe. If you get involved, get emotional, these guys will have us at their mercy."

She nodded. "If they hurt Joe…"

"They don't want to hurt Joe. But you and I are both going to have to be patient. This is a dance marathon, not a sprint. The longer it takes, the better. We can wear them down and keep Joe safe."

"How do you know they aren't going to hurt him?"

"They didn't even want to wake him up."

"That was more about them than it was for Joe."

She wasn't wrong, but she did give him an idea.

"We need to make them feel something for him," Mike said with a subversive laugh.

"You think that will work? That they will be that easily coerced?"

Love always had a way of making a person do

things that went against reason. He'd once heard that feelings were thoughts of their own and to negate and devalue feelings would only limit a person's intellectual abilities. In essence, to avoid feelings stunted a person.

He wasn't sure if he bought into the philosophy in its entirety—whenever he had been able to avoid feelings, it had been an asset rather than a hindrance—but then he could hardly be thought of as the perfect specimen of man. Regardless of his personal introspection, love could be the answer to most of life's problems.

"Helloooo? What in the hell! Did you hang up?" The man on the other end of the line spiraled into a full meltdown. "Rico, they effing hung up, man. How in the hell are we supposed to work with these people?"

Rico. The man had a partner named Rico.

Mike clicked off the Mute. "I'm right here. I was just trying to think of a solution to the problem with Joe." He paused.

"What problem?" the man answered, too quickly.

"Well, he is going to require a lot of care," he said, thinking about all the baby-related items he'd seen around Summer's house. "He is going to need a bottle, diapers, and someone to take dedicated care of him. Can you provide him with those basic necessities?"

There was a long pause. "You think I care if the baby eats?"

"You may or may not, but I think you are going

to care when he is crying because he's hungry." He turned to Summer. "What kind of formula does he drink?"

There was so much he didn't know about his son.

She nodded. "He has a sensitive stomach, so I can only use the formula from Costco, the one with the yellow lid."

Oh, this was going to be good. These guys clearly hadn't put a lot of thought into the actual logistical needs of taking care of a baby as young as Joe. And yet, that added level of need and dependence was going to also be what put Joe into additional danger. It took a lot to raise and care for a baby, and these guys knew maybe slightly less than Mike did.

"Did you hear Summer? The baby has special dietary needs. What can we do to get you the food Joe is going to need?"

"We don't need jack squat. If the baby cries, he goes outside. Plain as that." The man's voice sounded strained, as though even he knew that what he was saying was a bad idea. If someone heard a strange baby crying outside, that would pull in all kinds of attention. The only humans who would be pushed outside would be the kidnappers.

Mike paused, letting the lie sink into the man's psyche as he thought about the reality in which he had just placed himself. The expression "bit off more than they could chew" came to Mike's mind. But this was all good, all things he and Summer could use to buy time and even maybe to get to Joe all without giving the kidnappers the ransom they were asking for.

There was a rattle and the sound of a hand being placed over the phone as the kidnapper must have turned to his cohort, Rico. "Dude, do we have diapers? You know anything about where we can get some?"

Mike nearly laughed out loud as the bumbling kidnappers argued with one another about buying diapers at a gas station.

Summer covered her mouth as she nodded excitedly.

They had found the weak point in the other party's negotiation that would clear the barriers and give them the *in* that they needed.

"Look. I know you don't want to hurt the baby. That would land you in more trouble than I think you care to take on. So let us help you with him. We can bring you everything you need for Joe for the next two days, while we also work on getting you the codes. What do you think?" Mike hoped these idiots would see the advantage of keeping Joe well fed and looked after.

The man mumbled something Mike couldn't understand. "We are going to need some time. Let me talk to my people. We'll be in touch."

The phone line went dead.

Damn it. He hadn't meant to run the kidnapper off; all he had wanted to do was to get him to give them a little wiggle room.

He stared at the lit screen until it went dark.

There had to be something they could do, something that would help them take back control.

Chapter Ten

Hours later, Summer's phone rang and she hesitated to look at the Caller ID. Her only hope was that it was the kidnappers and they were coming back with a list of demands—demands that would bring Summer and Mike closer to getting their son back.

And yet, as she looked, she saw that it was her boss, Kevin Warble, from the DTRA. Luckily, as Mike glanced over at her phone from his seat next to her on her couch, all the screen said was Kevin. Mike couldn't know everything, not yet and maybe not ever. She had been doing the best she could, right up until her enemies had taken Joe. Now everything she had been trying to do, every safety precaution she had thought she'd had in place, was out the window.

She stood. "I'll be right back," she said to Mike, quickly making her way down the hall to her bedroom where she could find a little bit of privacy for the call that would now have to take place.

This one was going to hurt. She'd reached out to Kevin earlier when Mike was doing a perimeter check of the apartment complex after they'd received the ransom call.

Closing the door, she answered the phone. "Hey, thanks for getting back to me. I know you said you couldn't get me the codes, but there has to be something you can do. Something we can trade with these guys in order to get Joe back. Some innocuous codes. Anything…"

"Whoa. Let's not get ahead of ourselves. You know that isn't a possibility. Can you imagine if the code used by high-level, security clearance military engineers got into the hands of America's enemies? It would be a nightmare." Kevin sighed as though just the question of him getting her the codes exhausted him. "Have you had any other contact with the kidnappers?"

"No. Not yet. Have you had any luck tracking down the phone number or location of the device Rico and his buddy used to call?"

Kevin groaned. "Like we had assumed, it wasn't a number registered to any known phone. However, we have figured out the source app and have contacted the designers. They are looking into things to see if they can identify the phone assigned the number. But unfortunately, you know how all this goes. It's a waiting game."

"Did you guys manage to pull anything from any of the local cameras? Have you gotten any definitive answers?" she asked, begging for information about her son.

Kevin sighed. "I'm so sorry, Summer. All I can

tell you is that we're doing our best and we are trying to work as fast as we can. Just know that we are using every single thing we can to get Joe back."

She held no doubts he was telling her the truth, but it did nothing for the panic and terror she was feeling. Nothing would help calm her until she had Joe in the safety of her arms. She swallowed back the lump in her throat.

"I assume Mike is working on things from his side, correct?" Kevin continued.

"Yeah."

"Keep us apprised of any *issues* that may arise from his digging. We need to keep your role in the DTRA concealed—even from him. If not…well, you know how these things work. If you are exposed or your cover is blown, we are going to have to deny everything. You know what's at stake here, I hope."

Apparently, he meant beyond the scope of losing her son—the most important person in her life—she was also quite possibly going to lose her job and her freedom if her truth was uncovered.

Swell. Just swell.

Everything was falling down around her.

"I don't need you to tell me what else I have to lose. I'm more than aware. But right now, my main concern is the welfare of my son." Her anger pulsed within her and, for a moment, she wondered if it was misplaced and ill-advised for her to speak up, but at the same time she didn't care. "I think you calling me to tell me this is reprehensible. You promised to keep me and my son safe—and yet here we are and now you are threatening to throw me under the bus."

"I didn't mean it like that, Summer," Kevin said, contrite. "I just mean that you need to be careful with Mike. This is a tough situation, but know we are all working to fulfill our promises to you. However, you need to focus on doing your job."

Summer sighed. Maybe she was lashing out in the wrong direction. It was just…well, it was this inability to take direct action that was really killing her. All she wanted to do was to rush out, cut down the bad guys, and get her son back into her arms. And yet, all she could do was to sit in her apartment, make phone calls and wait for them to come to her. This powerlessness was unlike anything she'd ever felt before.

Not even being left at the altar compared.

And then there was that.

Here she was, forced to trust a man who had broken her heart and ripped out a piece of her soul once before. And already, he had allowed kidnappers to get to Joe. He'd only been back in her life for a matter of hours and he was destroying it all over again.

Logically, she wasn't angry with Mike. She couldn't be. Not really. The kidnappers had been targeting her; she had brought them to her doorstep. But she couldn't help the anger she was feeling from spilling over and tainting everything in her life.

Bottom line, she was angry with the world.

"Is there anything I can do beyond sit here and wait?" she asked, hoping Kevin would have something that could help staunch the roiling emotions threatening to destroy her.

"Like I told you earlier, the best thing you can do is stay exactly where you are. Get as much information about Rockwood as you can."

When she had been a child, she had been taught that if she was ever truly lost in a forest, the best thing she could do was just sit still—to stay where she was. Others would find her. And yet, this tore at the very cloth of her being. She wasn't a sit-and-wait kind of woman, especially in situations like this. She *had* to do something.

"Mike won't tell me anything. I need to start moving, to do something that will bring me closer to getting Joe back."

"Stop, Summer." Kevin's voice was rife with pity, and she hated it. "Let us take care of you. We have teams in place who are doing more than even I can tell you. Just give us time."

When she had signed her Department of Defense contract with the DTRA and taken the oath of office, there had never been anything about putting herself first. This was about her team and keeping them safe even if that meant putting the needs of her son and herself second. She didn't have to like it, but she had made the deal when she had taken the job.

She had known there would be sacrifices she would need to make when it came to being a DTRA agent, but she had never assumed her sacrifices would come in the form of her son's life.

She had been a fool to take this job on. She should

have just stuck it out with STRIKE and made it work. She'd loved her contracting world, but when things had gone haywire, she'd thought it had been the impetus she had needed to work full-time for the DTRA, which had led to her taking a position at Rockwood as a spy.

She'd thought she'd been making the right choice, making the best out of a bad situation and getting her life set up so that she could be a good mother while also being able to stand on her own two feet. But all she had done was make everything so much worse. She had fallen for the trap of greener grass in the hope of being a better provider. Guilt flooded through her. She should have just shut her mouth and done the job she had been paid to do for STRIKE, taken the money and gone home to her son. But no, and look where being a good person and doing the right thing had gotten her.

Why did being a good person, a good employee, and a good mother have to be such a juggling act? There was always one ball being dropped.

"You okay, Summer? Do you need anything from us, something I can have someone deliver? Maybe some dinner?" Kevin continued, breaking her train of thought.

"That's kind of you, but we'll be okay." She wasn't hungry and until now she hadn't even bothered to think about food.

"Okay, but let me know if you want or need anything. And I'll be in touch if we get any more leads."

"Thanks, Kevin. And hey, I appreciate all you're

doing." She sounded resigned, even to herself, as she ended the call.

When she walked out, Mike was holding a pizza box. "I hope you don't mind, but I thought you might be hungry."

What was it with everyone thinking that she needed to eat?

Summer nodded, giving him a weak smile as she forced herself to remember he didn't deserve to be the target of her rage. She followed him into the kitchen, where he set the pizza down and grabbed a couple of paper towels, handing her one. "Only the finest china for you, m'lady." He gave a little bow as she took the towel.

"Thank you, kind sir." She forced herself to curtsy as she played along, the small exchange reminding her of the dorkiness and quaint familiarity they used to have.

"And it is plain, just as you like it—thick crust and extra cheesy." He pulled out a chair at the island and helped her to sit before sitting next to her.

He remembered. The thought made some of the heaviness in her chest lift. He had made his mistakes and she had made hers, but there was such deep love between them. No matter what, they would always share an inexplicable bond; one filled with the nuances that came with familiarity and time.

This man still loved her, though it would never be the same love he had once felt for her—or the love she had once felt for him. They had now entered the world of love reserved only for those with the most broken of hearts.

He opened the box, the greasy scent of dough and butter filling the air and, doing so, making her stomach pang. She chuckled at the thought of how funny it was that others could sense things in her that she denied noticing in herself. Or maybe it was just that what she was really hungry for was the act of caring, a hunger Mike had filled, even without her so much as asking.

Mike was a good man.

She took a bite of the pizza as he made his way to the fridge and looked inside. It was exactly as she had remembered it, empty except for a few old beers, a bottle of mustard and some banana baby food she had forgotten to use up. He grabbed one of the beers, twisted off the cap and handed it over to her.

"No, I don't think I should." Summer shook her head slightly. In truth, she wanted the beer and the relaxation that it whispered of, but what if someone called about Joe?

She looked over at the clock. He should have been in bed right now.

Had they changed his diaper? Given him a bath?

At night, he loved to be rocked to sleep after a warm bottle. If they didn't do it, Joe would pitch a fit and, once he got started, and if he was overly tired, there was little anyone could do to calm him except to let him cry it out until he wore himself down and went to sleep on his own.

Anxiety pierced through her. What if they weren't

taking care of him at all? What if Joe was alone, unchanged and unfed?

Her breathing started to quicken as all the fears she held for Joe's safety filled her mind.

This wasn't going to be okay. Nothing was going to be okay. Things would never get back to where they had once been. And what was she doing about it all? Eating pizza. She was the worst mother ever.

"He is going to be okay, Summer." Mike spoke as though he could read her mind, or maybe it was that all of her thoughts were streaming on her face like it was a wide-screen television.

"How do you know, Mike? What if—"

"Stop. Don't swirl the drain of what-ifs. It does you and Joe no good."

He was right, but she hated to admit it. Without the what-ifs, she was left with only the reality of the situation—her son was in the hands of potential killers.

She took the beer Mike offered and took a sip.

"This is all going to be okay. We will get him back and they will take good care of him. A baby has a way of making everyone around them love them. I mean look at me," Mike said, sending her a wilting smile. "I love him. I loved him the moment you told me about him. That's all it took. And when I saw him, man…put a fork in me."

She smiled. "He is a handsome boy. And when he laughs, he laughs with his whole body in a way that makes you laugh too. I never thought I could love something as much as I love him."

"See what I mean? No one can walk by that boy and not fall for him. He is going to be safe if these men are at all partial to his charms; which, after our conversation with them, I think they are."

"We will see if they say the same thing in the morning; after he keeps them up all night. He likes to fall asleep with me, in my bed." Her eyes welled up with tears as she thought about the week after she had brought Joe home from the hospital. How hard she had tried to follow the rules she had read in the parenting books, chapters of which discussed the pitfalls of co-sleeping. In the end, instinct had taken over and she had given in to the needs of her baby over the opinions of a few.

Snuggling with Joe had become one of her favorite moments in her life. It was an incredible feeling to fall asleep with a baby, flesh of her flesh and bone of her bone. This little being who trusted her so much.

She had let him down.

Taking a long pull off the bottle, she thought about her mistakes. There had been so many in her life already, so many wounds, bruises, scrapes and scabs. It was really no wonder no one made it out alive.

"Mike, what did I do wrong with us? How did I push you away?" She put her beer down on the counter and started to play with the paper ring around the bottle's neck, pulling at the corners like behind it were the answers to life's questions.

He reached over and took her hand, interlacing their fingers. "Summer. Babe." He spoke the word like it was even more tender than his touch. "My problems that day… They really had nothing to do with you."

"Ah," she said with a forced laugh, hoping to diffuse some of the tension, "the old 'it's not you, it's me' line."

"You didn't do anything wrong. It wasn't you. It was me. I saw the future. I'd overheard Troy talking about a threat STEALTH had neutralized. A threat to us. To you. And I thought, *I can't do this*. I couldn't live a life with you, knowing I put you in danger. It was the hardest thing I ever did, walking away from that altar."

"You never told me…"

"I didn't think you would understand. You would have told me to push aside my fears and just follow through with the wedding. But I couldn't… I couldn't risk having you hurt or killed because of me."

He was right. She would have tried to convince him not to leave. But it wasn't him. It was her. What she had needed was a real, concrete answer…an aspect she could change in herself that would help her become stronger, better, and then never find herself in the same position again—and especially not with him.

"Do you think you will ever want to get married again?" he asked.

"To you?" She jerked, stunned by his question.

He let out a tight, surprised laugh. "Sure, or to whomever you love. Man, woman, alien…" he teased.

He had said "sure." Did that mean he was thinking about *them* becoming an *us* again? Could she handle something like that? Could she trust him with her heart after all the pain, confusion and misery he had put her through the last time?

If she said no, would she be doing a disservice to Joe? Probably. But if she said yes, would she be doing a disservice to herself?

"I don't know," she said, striking down the middle. This was one question better unanswered. "I guess I haven't really thought about it too much. I've been really busy for the last year or so." She sent him a smile to let him know that her words weren't meant as some kind of jab, but rather a truth masked in cotton. "And I've loved every second of it," she added.

"After we get Joe back, do you think I can get involved? I mean maybe we can figure out some sort of parenting plan or something. I don't want to step on your toes, but I can't imagine knowing that I have him and yet not having time with him. You know?" He looked slightly stricken at the thought.

Was his question about marriage directly related to his concern for being or not being in Joe's life? "If I get married, don't worry. You will always have a place. You are Joe's dad, and I want to give you every opportunity to be a part of his life as much or as little as you want. I will never stand in your way."

Even if they weren't destined to be together as a married couple, it didn't mean they weren't supposed to be together as parents. Raising Joe would require a collaborative effort and they would both have to give a little to make things work, but she was willing to do the work if he was.

"I just want what is best for Joe," he said.

"I agree. But I also think you coming and going in Joe's life will be hard." She paused. "So, if you are going to be in and out of his life when it's convenient for you, it's not going to be good for him. Before you commit to anything, I want you to really think about your options. With this, you are either all in or all out. No in-betweens."

He squeezed her hand as he listened, like he was already agreeing to her terms.

"Mike, this isn't going to be easy. I don't think you can possibly understand how hard parenting is going to be."

He smiled softly at her. "You know, I have always found the things in my life most worth having are never easy. Far from it." He moved her closer to him and lifted her hand to his mouth, softly kissing the back of her knuckles. "Those things that I have to struggle to attain are what I respect, love and cherish the most."

Ummm... What? Did he just tell me that he loved me? That he cherished me? I didn't even know he knew that word. What in the hell?

She couldn't read too much into his words or his actions. Nope. This had to be one of those times her imagination was playing tricks on her. Mike was the silent type. The type who rarely spoke the truths that lay in his heart. Then again, since they had reconnected, he had been more candid with her than he had been in nearly their entire previous relationship. Had he changed? Had he realized their communication was one aspect of their relationship that had been lacking, by both of them?

"Mike…" She said his name, the sound barely above a whisper. It instantly took her back to the many nights they had spent making love until they were exhausted and only sated when they found themselves engulfed in one another's arms.

Was that where this was headed? Was he making his move? Was he hoping she would take him to the bedroom? That they would make love?

She panicked and yet she didn't pull her hand away from his; she needed his touch. Tonight, of all nights, she wanted the support and love his being there provided. And, well, she wanted *all* of it, and him.

He helped her to stand and she took the lead, walking him slowly toward her bedroom. He had to have known what was coming next, just as much as she did, but he didn't seem to hesitate, though he also wasn't taking the lead. She liked that. He had normally always been the one to be the commander in the bedroom, taking what he wanted from her and leaving her so well pleased that she would collapse into a comatose-like sleep. Yet now he seemed almost passive, demure, in his want of her.

Or maybe he didn't want her?

No. She couldn't think about that—about being rejected by him for a second time, albeit maybe in a slightly less painful way.

Though, come to think of it, which was worse— having a heart or a body turned away?

Either way, it hurt.

She stopped outside her bedroom door. Questioning the step they were both about to take. "Mike—"

He stopped her by taking her lips with his, unexpectedly hurried but tender as he stole her words.

His tongue found the center of the bottom of her lip and she met him there. He pulled her close against his body and her hands moved down his sides. She could feel the bulge of his muscles underneath the fabric of his shirt. He still worked out. So many push-ups.

She grew weak at the knees, but she wasn't sure if it was because of his kiss or his body pressed against hers. It had been so long since she had been properly made love to.

Ben had been great, but he was nowhere near as good or as attentive as Mike had been to her when it came to between-the-sheets time.

She needed to feel Mike inside her, making love to her in the way only he could.

If they just had tonight and then things went back to the way they were, then fine. Whatever. But at least tonight they could forget about the reality that surrounded them, pushing in from all sides, and they could both just concentrate on the pleasure they could bring to one another.

For tonight, he could be hers and she could be his.

She melted into his kiss, letting him consume her soul as he took her lips. That feeling…that feeling of deep carnal bliss, oh…how she had missed that.

As he kissed her, it was easy to remember why

and how easily she had first fallen in love with this man. There was nothing as good or as satisfying as what he was making her feel right now.

She moaned and he opened his mouth slightly, letting her breath fill him as she hoped that he wanted to fill her.

"I want you." She slid her hands up, running her fingers through his thick hair and pulling his mouth hard against hers as he took in her words.

She moved them toward her bed, pushing away a box that was in the center of the room with her foot but still not breaking their kiss.

It had been so long since she had felt this way in his arms. And even in her wildest fantasies, she had never thought she would be back falling into bed with him.

He broke away. "You know I want you. This." He pressed himself against her. "You do things to my body…" He growled. "But I want to take care of you. And the last thing I want to do is screw up whatever is starting between us."

Logically, everything he was saying was sweet and thoughtful. She could even argue he was right, but it didn't staunch the way she felt or the need she had to feel him.

"Let's just see where tonight takes us." She tried to sound sultry, unconcerned, and far from the woman she really was—the mother who had a million worries on her mind.

Right now, all she wanted to do was to run away

from the truths of her reality with a man who had often taken center stage in her dreams.

Mike looked up at the ceiling, like the answers he was looking for were posted there. He should have known by now that when it came to their relationship—or whatever it was they were trying for here—there were no easy answers. They were both only left with questions.

He took her by the hand and led her to the bed. "Here, lie down."

Yes.

She did as he instructed, letting go of his hand as she scooted over to the other side of the bed—the side that had always been hers when they had been together.

He smiled as though he was thinking about the same things. He got into bed behind her and perched on his elbow as he looked at her. "Now, roll over."

She frowned at him, but he made a spinning motion with his hand.

"For now, I'm only going to rub your back. You need to get some rest. If this…this step in our relationship is something that you seriously want, it can wait. I am not going anywhere."

Chapter Eleven

He'd always had a special place in his heart for Summer, but damn if this woman wasn't going to kill him—she could be hard on a man. All he had wanted to do was to throw her down on that bed and make love to her until the morning sun broke into their reality. But those kinds of decisions led to ramifications he wasn't sure either of them was ready to face.

She was confused right now, hurting. As was he. But he hadn't been about to take advantage of her vulnerability, even if she had initiated the physical closeness, so he'd rubbed her back until she'd dozed off last night and then slept on the sofa. Or tried to. He'd spent most of the night tossing and turning, waiting for a call from the kidnappers. And he'd risen early to head out for breakfast, so she wouldn't have to make it or fret about not having much to offer.

Yes, he would have loved to have had a relationship with her, but if something went wrong—as things so often did in life, especially when she still had a chip on her shoulder about their past—he couldn't risk losing what he was hoping to have.

Wait. What was he hoping for, really?

He had told her all he wanted was for a functional, even good, parenting arrangement between them. But was that all he wanted? If they could go back to where they were and things went toward marriage again, he wasn't sure how he would react.

After last night and him putting a pin in her advances, he couldn't help but wonder if Summer would see his actions as just another rejection. He wouldn't blame her if she did. But she had to know that when it came to matters of the heart, he was a man who had to take things slowly. Sex was easy. Love was incredibly hard. And he had an awful habit of having sex turn into love and a need for a relationship.

They both couldn't give a relationship the attention it needed. Joe had to come first. Finding him had to come first. And God forbid something worse actually happened to Joe—and things didn't turn out like he wanted them to and he didn't make it out of this alive—they would never get over it. She would hate him. No. Before anything happened between them, he needed to get Joe back into the safety of their care.

Then they could worry about the rest of whatever was happening between them.

He walked into her apartment, carrying two cups of coffee and croissants. Hopefully she was awake. If not, he didn't want to rouse her. She needed some reprieve, but they also needed to be ready to hit the road. The kidnappers could call anytime now. And they needed to come up with something that would help stall them until they could be found and they could get Joe.

As he rounded the corner, he found her sitting at the kitchen island bent over her phone and scribbling on a notepad. "Hey. Where were you? I didn't think you were coming back," she said, her words coming out in a flurry of syllables surprisingly devoid of anger.

And there he had been, worried about his rebuff and her feeling rejected.

"I hope you don't mind. I borrowed your car. I just wanted to get us some food and you are woefully lacking in the pantry department." He set the bag on the counter in front of her and she dug in, taking a sip of coffee and opening the wrapper without even looking up at him. She started to scribble again, but he couldn't read what she was writing. "What are you working on?"

"Huh?" she asked, taking a bite.

"What happened to light this fire?" he asked, motioning toward the notes.

"Oh," she said, swallowing her bite. "I woke up and I had this idea and I did a little digging." As she spoke there was a strange inflection, like she was hiding something, but he didn't press.

"About?"

"Well, last night we told the kidnappers the best formula was the one with the yellow lid from Costco.

Complete the survey below and return it today to receive up to 4 FREE BOOKS and FREE GIFTS guaranteed!

FREE BOOKS GIVEAWAY
Reader Survey

1

Do you prefer stories with suspensful storylines?

○ YES ○ NO

2

Do you share your favorite books with friends?

○ YES ○ NO

3

Do you often choose to read instead of watching TV?

○ YES ○ NO

YES! Please send me my Free Rewards, consisting of **2 Free Books from each series I select** and **Free Mystery Gifts**. I understand that I am under no obligation to buy anything, as explained on the back of this card.

❏ Harlequin® Romantic Suspense (240/340 HDL GQ3J)
❏ Harlequin Intrigue® Larger-Print (199/399 HDL GQ3J)
❏ Try Both (240/340 & 199/399 HDL GQ3U)

FIRST NAME

LAST NAME

ADDRESS

APT.#

CITY

STATE/PROV.

ZIP/POSTAL CODE

EMAIL ❏ Please check this box if you would like to receive newsletters and promotional emails from Harlequin Enterprises ULC and its affiliates. You can unsubscribe anytime.

HI/HRS-520-FBG21

What if these guys actually listened and went there to get it?"

That seemed like a reach, but he didn't dare say that to her when she was feeling empowered in their hunt.

"I've been pulling security camera video—I got access from some contacts I have. I figure they have to have stayed in the area and there is only one Costco. The way I see it, even if they didn't get the formula there, at least it's a place to start. They're going to have to get baby food and diapers some-where. Basically, everything. And we know we are looking for a man named Rico, could be short for Richard or Ricardo or Enrico. Or not." She shrugged and waved the thought off like it was of no matter. "If we can nab a photo of these guys, we could get to them in a matter of hours. *If* we get lucky."

If was the keyword in that statement. There were millions of things that could go wrong with her plan.

"Did you find anything on the video?" he asked, motioning to her computer as he took a long drink from his coffee.

"I have seen a few potential suspects. I've cleared about thirty individuals so far. We have three we are going to have to look into a little deeper." She stuffed the rest of her pastry into her mouth and stood. She stuck out her hand like she wanted the keys to the car.

He handed them over and, finishing off his crois-sant, followed her out. He chewed fast, swallowing the last bite as he got into the car and buckled in. He had a feeling today was going to be a wild-goose chase, but it was a hell of a lot better than sitting around and playing the waiting game.

Summer headed south, well over the speed limit and barely slowing at the stop signs. "The first one on my list is a man named Cody. I found his picture and info in a search of public records—he was picked up for a DUI a year or so ago. He is in his midfifties and isn't married. He lives alone and works for the power company. So far as I can tell, there is no reason that he would need formula and baby wipes."

He could think of quite a few reasons the man would need something like that, but if this made her feel better, so be it.

"Did you hear anything from the kidnappers?" he asked, holding on to the "oh shit" handle above the passenger-side window as she nearly flew around a corner.

"No." She shook her head. "But I did call the number they contacted us from. Of course, it came back as busy and didn't go through. That was where I started when I couldn't find you." She glanced over at him and there was a strange guilty look in her eyes.

She was hiding something, but he had no idea what it could have been. Maybe she wasn't hiding anything and he was just seeing things that weren't really there. Maybe it was simply his own guilt for not being the man she needed that was leading him to read far too much into things with her. Or maybe he had lost some of his ability to look at her and know what she was thinking. It had been over a year since they had been this close.

"Anyhow, this Cody guy…" she continued, "he seems like the most promising of the leads I have so far. If we come up empty-handed, maybe our suspects just haven't hit the stores yet. But these guys will and, when they do, I'll be ready."

That was, unless they had actually been prepared to kidnap the baby and had gotten all their supplies in advance of taking any action. Any good team would have had everything planned out long before they'd taken any real action, and they'd have been overly prepared. But then again, the man they had spoken to last night had seemed at a loss when it came to babies.

"What are we going to do about the coding? What if we just hand it over?"

She looked at him like he'd lost his mind. "First of all, I don't have the code. Sure, I *had* it, but I don't keep that kind of information once I achieve my objective. I just pass it along to my team leader."

"Given the circumstances, don't you think they could work with us on this? Maybe give us some of the code and bury their own somewhere in it? We could use it to track them."

Summer nodded. "There isn't a chance. Besides, these guys are probably not the ones who want the code. In cases like these, when government secrets are involved, these kinds of ransom teams are normally only getting the information to sell it off to foreign governments or other bad guys. It would be stupid of them to use the codes for themselves."

He knew it was likely she was right, but they still needed some sort of leverage when it came to negotiations. If they didn't manage to get the drop on the men who held Joe, they needed to be ready to have something to trade. "What if we prepared some dummy code? Worst case, we don't use it."

She slowed the car, but only slightly. "Maybe I can get my team leader to help, but my crew would probably be starting from scratch. Who knows how long it would take." She sounded dejected, as if she already knew the idea wouldn't work.

He hated when she sounded like that, resigned to failing. "You never told me what the code was actually for."

"Does it matter?" she countered.

He pursed his lips. "Yeah. It could. I have a team we can turn to, as well. You know Zoey is amazing with tech. My teams at STEALTH, if given the information, can set to work. That way we have all of our bases covered. Consider it our contingency plan."

She nibbled at her bottom lip.

"You need to tell me the truth. If you want, it never has to leave this car, but I need to know why this is all so important to these people. If I don't know what is motivating them, then I can't know what they are willing to lose in order to get what they want. And the last thing I want is for them to get to a point in which they are so desperate that they are willing to hurt Joe. I would never be able to get over something like that."

She sighed. "How much do you know about Con-Flux?"

"All I know is what Zoey and my team at STEALTH have told me."

Summer scowled as she looked at him. "You can trust me, Mike. I hope you know that."

He hated the way she was making him feel right now. They both knew secrets weren't something that could be shared between them, not really. If he gave her sensitive information, it could end up with both of them being killed—possibly even by their own teams. If they told secrets, they were a liability. Whatever they said to one another, no one could ever know. It would be the greatest exercise in trust that either of them could ever participate in with one another—was he willing to take the leap of faith?

If he opened up to Summer, he would not only be putting himself at risk, but also his team—a team that contained his siblings. As much as he loved Summer, he could never put one of his siblings in that kind of position.

"You know I can't—"

She stopped him with a sideways glance. "I get it. But what I'm about to tell you could get me into a whole lot of trouble. I need you to be on the same page as me…and we need to get Joe back. No one outside of this car has to know what we say to one another. But you need to know some truths, and so do I. This is all about Joe."

He squirmed in his seat. If she told him something, anything that put him in danger with his team… "I don't think—"

"Stop. I know what you are going to say," she said, her words coming out at a mile a minute. "But here's the deal. If I don't tell you who you are working for, and you continue on, you may find your guys get in deeper than you ever thought possible." She nibbled at her lip, like she was pausing to weigh the ramifications of what she wanted to tell him.

"What in hell are you talking about, Summer?"

She slowed her speed a little more. "ConFlux and its late CEO were working for the DOD."

He had known that the company had been taking military contracts, so her information wasn't much of a surprise. Yet her opening up to him made him clench. Something felt *off.* "Summer, stop."

"Don't worry, I already scanned my car for bugs. My phone is in a Faraday bag. Put yours in, too." She motioned toward the desert khaki bag between them. He did as she instructed. "Now, stop worrying. Just listen. You need to have an idea of what we are up against."

He set the Faraday bag back on the console between them. Of course, she would think about their safety. She'd likely had this conversation all planned out long before he had even gotten back with their coffees.

"Okay, but I don't want whatever it is you are going to tell me to—"

"Get you in trouble?" She finished his sentence, her words coming fast.

"That's one way to put it," he said.

"I'm trusting that whatever I tell you remains between us." She locked eyes with him. "Can I trust you?"

He paused, thinking about all the implications that making such a promise would mean. If he agreed, he would be putting her before his family and before his team. "You know I care about you, that I want to know what you have to tell me, but you can't ask this of me."

"I am not asking you to compromise yourself, just to listen."

He wasn't sure she could have one without the other, but he didn't bother to argue. When Summer had her mind set on something, there was nothing that was going to stop her. The last thing he wanted to do was to be the one who would delay them from getting their son back. If she needed him to be on this team for the good of their spontaneous family, then he needed to get on board. Joe first, consequences second.

Mike gave a slight nod, motioning for her to continue.

"ConFlux doesn't just machine parts for the government. They also work in tech that is unknown by most of the public. In the early 2000s, they started working for the DOD, machining parts for fighter jets and then UAVs. But since then, those technology systems have started to take a back seat to other, more *dynamic* technologies."

Working overseas, he'd witnessed more than his fair share of dynamic technologies. When he'd been on patrol, he had seen everything from old car batteries used as bombs to tech that could sense vibrations on house windows and tell him what the people inside were saying. What, exactly, Summer was talking about could have a million different definitions, and he wasn't sure he wanted to know specifics. At least, he wasn't sure he wanted to ask and be drawn further into the web she was weaving.

He held his tongue.

She checked him, and her expression soured slightly as though she knew exactly what he was thinking. "The code that was taken was for some of these dynamic technologies."

"What would the kidnappers within Rockwood want to do with it if they got their hands on the information?"

She looked away from him. "Well, that is where I'm a little foggy. I'm not sure whether or not this code would be kept by them or sold. And if it was to be sold, which I think is more likely, I don't know if it would be to foreign governments or traded domestically."

"Why would someone in the States want code for tech that was built for the US military?"

Summer smiled wickedly, like she was proud he had sniffed something out. "The DOD assigns governmental contracts to only a select handful of companies. These contracts can be extremely lucrative. In essence, this could be a case of corporate espionage—some other US company could be employing Rockwood to get the information so they can undercut ConFlux to gain control of the limited government contracts. But this is all just a hypothesis."

Holy crap. He'd had no idea. This information could change everything.

And he couldn't tell a single soul.

He dropped his head into his hands as he tried to make sense of everything she was saying. For now, the only certainty was that he had to know more about what Summer had gotten herself wrapped up in. "What kind of tech is this code actually for?" he asked, a sickening lump forming in his stomach.

She chewed on her bottom lip. "It is used in the making of IGS—Information Gathering Systems."

"Such as?"

She switched on her blinker, slowing as she turned down a side road leading to their primary suspect's residence. "They have been helping build nanotechnology the size of bugs and smaller, which can be deployed in a variety of mission settings from combat to civil unrest. Basically, it's used in building the proverbial flies on the wall. This tech can also be used, however, with whatever chemical weaponry they deem necessary."

He tried to control the shock that was undoubtedly marking his face. ConFlux had been profiting from the world of nano warfare. He'd heard whispers of tiny devices that were information collection bugs.

There had been talks in Congress sometime in 2009 about such things, but he had yet to have heard of or seen them actually being built or deployed en masse.

The result of such devices being employed on the battlefield and in intelligence gathering was almost unimaginable. It was potentially as life-changing as bringing the internet to the public. Once this IGS technology was released, everything would change. There would no longer be any safe place. Everywhere and everyone could be compromised.

And now, the code to create the technology was at the center of their war to get their son back. They couldn't allow anyone to get their hands on the code—not when it had such potentially cataclysmic ramifications for the world—but they also had to do something to save their baby.

Chapter Twelve

Though Summer had promised herself she wouldn't compromise Mike by giving him information he shouldn't be privy to, she had done exactly that. But the DTRA and Kevin were doing little to help Joe, and she needed answers and she needed them fast. As far as she could tell, she would only get them by bringing Mike into her inner circle. Sure, she could potentially lose her job if they found out she had divulged government secrets, but right now she trusted Mike far more than anyone else.

No one cared about Joe as much as they did. No one would fight as hard as they would. Kevin had proved just that by blowing her off and telling her to just sit still when her son's life was at stake. If he found out about what she'd told Mike, he only had himself to blame.

She pulled her car to a stop about a half a block from their first suspect's house. The man was nowhere to be seen, but that didn't mean he wasn't inside with Joe, holed up like the criminal he potentially was while he waited for the ransom demands to be delivered. Well, he could keep waiting; she was done playing Rockwood's games. Right now, she was the one in control, hunting down the people who wished her and her loved ones harm.

This was her game now.

She glanced over at Mike; he looked at odds with everything. She didn't blame him.

He'd always had the power to bring her back to reality and make her feel like she was nineteen years old and completely adrift. Had she told him too much? Was he thinking she was a security liability to him? Was he thinking she was untrustworthy? Had she made a mistake in telling him anything?

Damn, she needed to get out of her head. But ever since she had dropped the info bomb, Mike had been silent. No doubt, he was thinking about all the things she'd said, piecing it all together with whatever his group already knew. He was also probably thinking about how he was going to tell Zoey and his teams at STEALTH about this newly acquired information.

She didn't want him to go to them with the details, but at the same time, she was almost sure it would be exactly what he would do.

"The nanotech they are working on right now at ConFlux is called Mayfly." She felt bad feeding him a fake code name, but if she heard it from another outside source, she would know if Mike and the STEALTH team used it.

Here was hoping she never heard the code name Mayfly again.

She hadn't wanted to bring Mike in this deep, but

the people who had taken Joe had struck low and had left her with no other cards to play. She'd had to call him in; he was one of the only people she knew she could trust. At least with him, she could understand his motives and his driving forces. Understanding those meant she also understood his weaknesses— and his strengths. And right now, she needed every strength he bore as she was barely able to process a single thought. If he proved himself, she would tell him the whole truth. Maybe.

Though she understood that what was happening, and her inability to focus, was due to her emotional state, it didn't mean she could control their effects on her mental state. She had been trained to be mentally resilient and deal with stress, but no one had prepared her for a situation like this. Was she strong enough to do what needed to be done? What if she failed? What if Joe ended up getting hurt—or worse?

Her breathing quickened.

One step at a time. One task at a time. That's all she could focus on right now. Anything else and she would lose whatever ground she had managed to gain in her search.

Resilient. I have to be resilient.

This step was all about their suspect. If they got lucky, Joe would be inside the gray house with the white covered porch just down the street. Joe would be fine. He would be gurgling and cooing inside with this Cody guy and Rico, who would prove not to be monsters but merely instruments of the bosses who employed them to do their bidding.

Here was hoping. And here was hoping Mike didn't figure out she was still keeping things from him. If he did, he would likely never trust her again.

"Let's head over there, see if we can get a bead on Joe. If he is in there, we will bust down the door." She ran her hands over her face as she thought about calling Kevin again and telling him where she was and what they were doing. No. He didn't need to know she was going against orders. She was an agent for the DTRA and sometimes being an agent meant she had to go a little rogue.

Mike pulled out his phone from the Faraday bag and started to text someone. Was he already telling Zoey about the nano secrets she had shared? Was he telling her about Mayfly?

Summer stopped her thoughts before she let out a resigned and pained sigh. This, trusting Mike, would be a test.

"You ready?" she asked, grabbing her phone out from the Faraday bag.

By the time they got done here, it was likely that STEALTH would know all about the inner workings of ConFlux and their secret work for the Department of Defense.

He slipped his phone into his breast pocket as he looked over at her. "Let's stick together. No matter what happens, we can't split up. I don't want to lose sight of you. Got it?"

She nodded as she looked around. The neighborhood was quiet. It seemed as though everyone in the area was either at work or at school; there wasn't even a dog outside sniffing around. In fact, if she was forced to describe it, she would have said it was eerily devoid of any evidence of life. How was it possible that there wasn't even a bird fluttering around, picking at bugs?

The words "calm before the storm" came to mind.

Well, they were that storm.

She smiled to herself as she stepped out of the car and Mike followed. He walked beside her on the sidewalk. "Hold my hand," she said, extending it toward him.

If they wanted to be ignored, the best thing they could do was to look like a happy, normal couple.

He slipped his hand into hers and, as he did, she thought of the way his fingers had felt on her back as he had loved her last night. The memory made her want to sink into him, to let the warmth of his embrace lull her into a sense of comfort, but they weren't what they used to be and she would be foolish to think otherwise.

Without realizing it, she mirrored his walk and they moved in sync. Just another of the subtle body language cues that bespoke a happy couple. It was strange how their bodies had such incredible muscle memories when it came to each other—and especially their hearts.

She could so easily imagine falling back in love with him. And as she realized it, she wondered if she had ever really fallen out.

They moved toward the house, strolling along.

The suspect's driveway was empty, but there could be a car parked in the garage.

The gray house sat back from the road, its yard in desperate need of a mow. Weedy flowers poked up through tall grasses as they angled for the sun. The blades of grass brushed against the cuff of her pants, making a scratching sound that she doubted she would have normally noticed, but now sounded as loud as a semitruck barreling down a dirt road.

Nearing the door, they could hear the sound of techno music playing inside, the noise thick with rhythm but devoid of anything Summer would have considered enjoyable. She sent Mike a glance. From the quirk of his brow, she could tell he was thinking something similar.

"Apparently, we are walking up on Studio 54 here," he joked.

"You think he has glow sticks and bottled water for us when we join the party?"

Mike chuckled. "Just the thought of what it must be like in that house makes me worry about catching some kind of communicable disease."

"The only thing I think we are going to have to worry about catching from this guy is a case of being chronically single."

He started to laugh, the sound a bit too loud and out of place, and he clamped his mouth shut.

She stopped at the front door. The music rattled the windows and, from where she stood, she spotted a worn leather couch and a forest-green recliner perched in the man's living room. The floor was cluttered with spent candy wrappers and take-out boxes, but there was nothing to indicate their baby was inside.

"Let's walk around back," she said, making sure that they were still, as of yet, unnoticed.

Mike hopped down from the porch step, holding out his hand to help her. As she stepped down, she let go of his hand. She wanted to go for her gun, to be ready in case something went sideways here, but she talked herself off that ledge.

If the man inside saw them stalking around his house with their guns raised, there was no way she could talk herself out of the situation. Someone would undoubtedly get hurt, and the last thing she wanted to do was to put Joe into a situation in which he was in even more danger. Not to mention how things would play out with Kevin.

She needed to fly just under the radar here.

They moved quickly around the side of the house, slipping through the wooden fence's gate, silently clicking the lock open and making sure to keep it slightly ajar in case they needed to make a quick exit.

Her body tensed as they moved toward the back wall of the house, careful to stay out of sight from anyone who may have been inside. Hopefully the guy was alone or with only his accomplice, as she had assumed. While she was reasonably proficient with a gun, it wasn't typically her style to put herself into a situation where it could turn into a Wild West shoot-out. She was more of a "stick to the shadows and take them out at their proverbial knees" kind of woman.

Mike raised his fist in the air, motioning for her to stop. His body rested on the wall beside the sliding-glass door. His hand lowered to his weapon, readying for the threat, but as he peeked around, his hand moved off his gun and up to his face. Moving back to his position, hidden by the wall, he glanced over at her. His body was convulsing with silent laughter.

"What?" she asked, wondering what the hell had gotten into him.

"This is definitely not our dude."

"But…he was buying formula and diapers. And he had a history of working overseas and in the Sandbox. Are you sure?" She frowned. The hope she hadn't known she had been feeling twisted down her chest and pooled at her feet like spent tears.

"You have to see this. Seriously," he whispered. He stepped in her direction so they could switch positions on the wall and she could glance inside.

As she moved around him, she tried to remind herself that she'd known this was a thin lead from the moment she had discovered the man. She had been grasping at straws; she couldn't be disappointed now when it quite possibly would lead to nothing.

She leaned around the door frame and peered inside. It took her a minute to make sense of the scene in front of her. There, standing in the middle of what would have been a dining room in most homes, was a man in his midfifties. Around him was a series of white, lattice-style baby gates. The floor was covered with a zoo-animal-patterned blanket. The dining room had been transformed from the heart of the household, where most families had dinner chats and meetings, into a makeshift playpen.

Her gaze moved to the man. His chest was exposed; a pacifier was laced on a string around his neck. He wore an adult diaper and a pair of duck slippers. Sitting beside the man was a bottle and a can of the yellow-lidded baby formula.

What in the hell had they walked into?

She had always thought she was open-minded and relatively nonjudgmental, but standing there staring at this man-baby, she was utterly shocked. And angry. Angry because she'd wanted this to be a kidnapper, wanted to find Joe, and he wasn't there.

In her wildest dreams, she had never seen anything even remotely close to the scene in front of her. And though she was aware she should look away—that they should bug out and get as far from this as possible, and get back to their hunt for Joe—all she could do was stare.

The grown man dressed as a baby sat, blissfully unaware he was being watched. He reached to his left and picked up his cell phone like he was recording himself. He made gurgling sounds and popped the pacifier into his mouth.

Wow.

There was a tug on the back of her pants as Mike pulled her away from the door. "You agree this isn't our guy?"

She nodded, unable to put words to the flurry of thoughts and feelings she was experiencing.

Mike took her hand, a smile on his face. "If all your leads are this *interesting*, we are going to have one hell of a day."

Chapter Thirteen

Back in the car, all he could do was look down the road at the unassuming gray house and laugh. "Summer, that has to be one of the craziest things I have ever seen in my damned life." His words sputtered out from between guttural laughs.

Damn, it felt good.

She covered her mouth with her hands, seemingly embarrassed by the situation in which they had found themselves. "I swear, I had no idea. I just put the pieces together. Something was off." She started to giggle.

"Oh, I can totally understand how this guy would raise some red flags and how you would want to check him out, but *damn*." He roiled with laughter as he thought about the man standing in the middle of a baby-gate playpen dressed like an oversize baby.

He had heard of infantilism, but…just *wow*.

"I… That…" Summer giggled. "Did you…?"

"Oh, I saw what was going on in there. That was… wow." Their words filled the spaces between their laughter as they tried to make sense of exactly what they had stumbled upon.

Tears started to streak down Summer's face as her giggles turned to full-blown roaring laughter. "That…is…the best…thing… I've ever seen…in my life."

For what must have been five minutes they sat in the car and laughed. Though it was one of the strangest things he had experienced, Mike was grateful. It had been so long since they had laughed together like this, and the tension of the kidnapping had seemed to push away the possibility of laughter until they got Joe back. This, these moments lost in the throes of joy, he wanted a life of with her.

He wiped the tears from the corners of his eyes then reached over and ran his thumb across Summer's cheek. "If nothing else, I feel like I need to thank you for that. Seriously," he said, gaining control over his aching gut, "I will never forget that as long as I live. That was amazing."

She dipped her head, moving her face deeper into his palm. "I aim to please."

"That, that right there, is something I know all about. You are by far the best woman I have ever met for that, and many other reasons." The words spilled out of him without his really thinking about it, but as they dripped from his lips, Mike suddenly felt embarrassed.

He shouldn't have said that, not right now, and maybe not ever. They were already treading on treacherous ground when it came to their feelings toward one another and any possible future they could have; he shouldn't be making it any more complicated by opening up to her like he just had. It was just, with levity filling the air had come the desire to be tender and honest. And Summer had opened up to him…she had trusted him with her secret. That had to mean *something*, didn't it?

She reached up and touched the hand that still rested on her face. "Before I had Joe, I always thought you were the greatest gift in my life. I was right, but then you ended up giving me a greater gift than I could have ever imagined. If that is all we ever get to have together, then I will consider my life blessed. You…you made me a mother."

His body drove him toward her and he took her lips with his.

Damn. He loved this woman so much. There were so many reasons not to kiss her, not to take this step or go down this road with her again, but he couldn't stop himself.

Besides, he could love a friend, and friends kissed…right?

She reached up and ran her fingers through his hair, pulling him closer to her, like she couldn't get enough. This. Her. It was all so *hot*.

But they couldn't. No.

Not right now. Possibly, not ever.

He removed his hand from her face as he leaned away, breaking their kiss. "I'm glad to have you back in my life. I don't know how I survived without you…and your friendship."

The light in her eyes flickered and dulled. "My friendship," she said, her words equal parts question and pain. "Yeah."

He didn't know what to do to make the light in her eyes reappear, but he wanted it back. She reached down and started the car, effectively putting an end to the moment, and it pained him. He put his hand on hers as she reached for the gearshift. "Summer, you know I never stopped caring about you."

She pulled her hand away. Putting it on her knee, she tweaked the fabric of her pants. "You can't do this to me." She sighed and looked down at her fingers.

"Do what?" he asked, not exactly sure which "this" she was referring to.

"I can't get my heart broken by you again. It hurt too much last time. I was stupid for thinking we could take things to the bedroom last night. I regret it. I shouldn't have even made that an option. At least, not yet." She sounded as if she was at odds with herself.

"Not yet? Does that mean you think there could potentially be something between us? Beyond co-parenting?" he asked, not sure if he should press her with questions.

"Our co-parenting arrangement needs to come first. Joe. He needs to come first." She pulled her hands into fists and then opened her fingers. "There are so many things going on right now... I'm afraid if we kiss again—if we do *whatever*—that we will both come to realize it was a mistake. And there is no going back. I don't want to relive the past."

He knew all too well about wanting to redo the choices he'd made in his past. His thoughts flashed to the agony on her face the moment he had told her that he couldn't marry her. If there was one moment he would want to take back, that was it.

Things could have been so different.

"You're right, Summer," he said, yielding to their complicated reality and the validity of her words. "I'm sorry. I shouldn't have kissed you."

"You didn't see me pushing you away." She smiled gently, looking over at him. "I—*we*—just have to both be strong and do what is right. At least, right now."

He had to find solace in the fact she had left the door slightly ajar, just enough for him to slip into her life and perhaps someday find a relationship. But he held no hope it would be the same as before, or that it would even really happen.

For now, he just needed to be in the moment.

"What other leads do you have?" he asked, trying to pull himself out of the heaviness of the air that surrounded them. "Please tell me that we have another diaper-wearing man to look into," he teased. "That was unforgettable."

She laughed, the sound sprinkled with stress. "I'm sorry. I never— Again, I had *no* idea."

"Oh, don't apologize for that. It was awesome." He laughed. "We need to find Joe, but part of me wants to go back and get pictures of that dude. Troy and AJ would get a kick out of that." He took his phone from his pocket, about to text his family.

"What are you doing?" All the laughter was stripped from Summer's voice, catching him off guard.

Why would she care who he was texting? Was she jealous?

"I was just going to tell the fam about the dude. They are going to laugh so hard."

She frowned, but nodded slightly. "Ah, okay."

Something was off, but he wasn't sure what he was picking up on—the weirdness of their relationship or something else.

"You want me not to tell them?"

She smiled, the action forced and false. "You know that if I see them again, they will tear into me for taking you there."

"Nah, they are cool like that. If anything, they're going to be jealous they didn't get to witness it firsthand." He laughed, the sound as off as her smile.

Her phone vibrated and she retrieved it. "Hello?" she said, answering.

He looked out the window as she put the car into gear and they started to slowly drive away from the man whom neither would forget.

"Any leads?" she asked, her sentence clipped.

He couldn't make out the words coming from the other end of the line; all he could hear was the timbre of a man's voice. It must have been someone she worked for. And then a thought struck him... she didn't work for STRIKE and she'd said she *had* worked for Rockwood, but who did she work for now? Who was on the other end of the phone, feeding her information and asking her questions?

He tried to check himself before he grew suspicious of Summer or read too much into what was happening. She had told him more than he could have asked for. If she hadn't told him something, it was for a reason. He didn't have to like it, but his life was also cloaked in secrecy, and he had to accept their reality. He, too, was limited in what information he could share, and with whom.

She glanced over as he looked at her, guilt flashing across her features.

Could she tell what he was thinking?

He turned, looking out the passenger-side window as they drove toward the highway.

He couldn't get sucked into the endless confusion of questions and second-guesses. He could be aware, but he couldn't force Summer to do anything or to tell him anything she wasn't ready to tell him.

In the meantime, he could wait—as long as it didn't interfere with their finding Joe.

"Sure," she said to the person on the other end of the line. "Thanks." There was a flatness to her voice.

She dropped her phone on top of the khaki bag sitting between them on the console.

He wanted to ask her who she had been talking to and what was going on, but he held back. She would open up to him when and if she wanted to. Until then he had to be patient.

"Who else did you want to look into?" he asked, trying to make the look of disappointment lift from her face.

"The next one on my list doesn't quite fit the profile we are looking for." She seemed to forget about the phone call on purpose, like she didn't want him to think anything about it.

Fine, two could play the ignore-the-obvious game.

"This time I have a lead on a man and a woman," she continued. "From the video I pulled, it appeared they were having a tense discussion in the formula aisle before getting the brand we recommended. They have no child on record and the man is on the federal watch list."

How would she know who was on the federal watch list? Was it possible that she was now working for the government?

Some of the pieces seemed to click into place.

"I'm sure your team has a pretty good idea of what they are doing and who they are looking for, but it seems to me that most new parents have probably had some kind of fight in the middle of Costco."

She laughed. "You have me there. You're probably right."

If he kissed her again, would she open up? They had put a pin in anything between them, but damn, he was tempted to try to make her forget herself again.

He thought of Troy and Kate. Kate worked for the FBI. Maybe he could make a call and she could get in touch with her people in the Bureau and they could look into Summer and find out who she worked for and maybe even why. And yet, the idea made an empty thud within him. He didn't want to have to do this kind of digging on the woman who had been such a big part of his life for so long.

Here Summer was, bringing him into her life with one open hand while pushing him away with the secrets she held in the other. Frustration filled him and a grumble slipped from his lips.

"What's the matter?" Summer asked.

He wanted to unleash the truth, to tell her all the things he was thinking, and then at the same time he wanted to rise above it all and not give in to the swirling mess of his thoughts and feelings.

"Summer, can I ask you something?" he said, glancing over at her.

"Sure," she said, but she didn't sound it.

"Something is bothering me about you, and I don't want you to get upset, but I need to make sense of a few things. Okay?" he asked, hating that he was going to have to take a roundabout to get to the truth of who she had become and why.

She slowed the car, but didn't stop driving. "Shoot."

He nodded, almost unconsciously. "So, you told me that things went south with STRIKE and you went to work for Rockwood. You don't work for them anymore. Yes?" he asked, treading lightly.

"Yep." She gripped the wheel tight, pulled the car over to the side of the road and put it in Park. Letting go of the wheel, she stared over at him. She opened her mouth like she was going to speak, but stopped. She motioned as if to speak three times before she made a sound. "I know what you are getting at. And I'm not as good at this as you are."

Had she meant for her words to be a jab? He wasn't sure what "this" she was talking about and he wasn't sure he would like it once he did, but he had to know.

"Good at what, Summer?"

She stared at her hands like they held the answers. "Did you tell your family about Mayfly? Did you tell anyone?" Her tone made him feel like he was the one on the spot and not her.

"I didn't. I wouldn't. You asked me not to. Why do you ask?" He made sure there was not a single twang of falseness in his voice; she didn't need to read anything into him that wasn't there. Right now, she had to be looking for anything to keep her feet out of the fire. "I wouldn't betray your trust, never again."

He could see her mouth form words and her eyes take on the storm that came with a fight, but just as quickly as the tempest started, it receded. She gave a resigned sigh. "I just needed to make sure you won't betray me, and that you know I will never betray you, Mike. I couldn't just run headfirst into this thing, whatever it is, without first doing some checking into you."

"Uh-huh." He crossed his arms over his chest and leaned back in the passenger's seat as he waited for the rest of her storm to play itself out. He tried not to be hurt by the fact she hadn't trusted him and she'd run a background check. If anything, he should have been flattered that she would go to that much work to have him in their lives. "And what did you find?"

"Nothing so far, but I'm still looking." She

watched him as if she could find the answers she was looking for in his features.

"You mean *your team* is looking into things." His words sat sour on his tongue.

She cringed, the motion so subtle that if he hadn't been looking for it, he would have likely missed it.

"Yes, my team."

"You gonna tell me about who you are working for, or are you going to make me drag it out of you, Summer?" he asked.

She tapped her fingers on the steering wheel. "I'm not trying to be difficult, Mike. I swear." She paused, collecting herself. "You know if I tell you, I could be further compromising your safety and mine. Don't you think I've already compromised you enough, given the amount of information I've already shared?"

"I'm in the fray. You can't stop talking to me now."

"But will it make a difference if you know who I'm working for? Will it matter in getting Joe back?"

She had him there. "Based on this," he said, lifting the Faraday bag for her to see, "you must be working for a group made up of a lot of initials. I need to know how much trouble I'm going to be in if it comes out that I'm working with you. So, which alphabet soup organization is it? Please tell me that you are working for the government and not another group like Rockwood."

Her mouth fell open with shock. "No. No. I'm not working with the bad guys. It's nothing like that."

This woman was in deep. Only how deep was yet to be discovered.

"Did you come to Missoula just to meet up with me?"

She didn't meet his eye.

"So, yes?"

"I needed someone I could rely on." Her words were charged with emotion. "You were the only person I knew with connections to Rockwood who wouldn't know I had infiltrated the group. I needed information, but I also needed to stay in the shadows. My boss wants me to find out how much Rockwood had ended up pulling from ConFlux after I gave them the keys."

"Who are you working for, Summer? You have to tell me."

"The man on the phone was my boss at the DTRA. I've been an agent for them for the last twelve months. They have been great."

"The DTRA?" He was familiar with a lot of the acronyms within the federal government, but this wasn't one of them.

"The Defense Threat Reduction Agency. We are a part of DARPA. Technically, I'm working remotely out of an outpost connected to the New Mexico office."

DARPA, he had heard of; it had been created during the Manhattan Project. Did that mean she was working with weapons of mass destruction? "Holy hell, Summer. Are you working with nuclear weapons?"

"I'm not—at least, not right now." She shook her

head. "Right now, I'm still working on low-level threat assessments and implementing effective neutralization strategies."

"So, let me get this straight…you are the one who finds 'threats' and then calls in teams to wipe them out?" He frowned as he tried to make sense of what she was saying.

"In layman terms, yes." She nodded. "And to answer your next question, yes, the DTRA is the reason I was working with Rockwood. Like I said, I had been infiltrating their company. Basically, Rockwood should have gotten nothing. It's why I needed you. Why I've been asking you about Rockwood. Do you know if they know my real identity? Have I been exposed?"

"Do you think they found out about your being a double agent and they connected the dots?"

"It's the only reason I can think of for why they are coming after *me* for the codes. I mean, why else would they target me—Joe?"

"Damn, Summer. Just… *Damn*…" He sounded breathless even to himself.

She put the car into Drive and merged back into traffic. "You can say that again. But I'm still not sure how they figured out that I was a double agent. There were a few times they might have found out, but the links would have been thin. I mean, how would they know I had access to any of the codes, codes I sent to my boss? For all Rockwood should have known, I only broke into the network. That was it. They shouldn't have known about any codes."

They sat in silence as she made her way onto the highway. He had no idea where they were going, but he didn't bother asking.

He chuckled as he watched her. "You do know how cool you are, right?"

She jerked slightly as she looked over at him. "What? What are you talking about?"

"Really. You may actually be one of the coolest chicks I know." He gave an amazed laugh. "Here I was, thinking that you had totally just screwed up your life and gotten yourself into major crap without intending to. And yet, I was wrong."

"No, you're not wrong. I definitely got myself into some major crap." She sent him a coquettish smile.

"Yeah, but what happened was entirely outside of your control. You didn't know these people would infiltrate your family and steal Joe as a result of your work," he offered, hoping that his support would help rid her of any guilt she may have been feeling. She had only been doing her job. Nothing more. "So, explain the thing with Ben. Do you think it was him who sniffed out your identity?"

"He is smart, but I don't think he did. I was so careful around him. My team at DTRA ran strong cover for me. Like I said, I don't think he is the one behind the kidnapping or them asking for the ransom to be paid in the stolen code. I think he came to my apartment to win me back, and saw you. He was just hurt and angry. He is jealous."

Just because she didn't think Ben was behind Joe's disappearance, it didn't mean Mike would stop hating the dude. If anything, he wanted to punch him in the face more now than ever.

"Does Ben still work for them?" he asked.

She nodded.

Yep, he hated him. But sometimes two people didn't need to like each other to find common ground. "What if you called him? Do you think he could help lead us to Joe? Maybe he knows what they did with him."

She smiled. "I don't know…but that is a good idea, after all. I know I rejected it at first. Maybe he has someone he can go to. He loved Joe, too, you know."

The words burned at him, but he tried to cover them with the salve of possibly getting some much-needed answers. "I'm glad. Joe needs to have as many people in his corner in life as possible."

Yeah, being a parent was going to be one heck of a kick to the ass if these last few days were any kind of preview of what was to come. Underprepared and overwhelmed didn't even begin to encompass all the feelings he was having about becoming a father to this little boy. However, it came with the knowledge that when something involved his son, he would do whatever it took to make sure he was safe—even if that meant putting himself in dangerous and uncomfortable situations…with or without a grown man dressed up as a baby.

"Summer, you are having a hell of a big life." He smiled over at her. "I'm proud of you for making the best out of a bad situation. And again, I'm sorry I forced the change upon you."

She met his smile with her own. "I'd be lying if I said it has been easy, but at the same time, I have to admit that since we split, I have done a lot. I'm proud of how far I've come. How much I've learned. You forced me to grow in ways I never thought possible, and for that I can be grateful."

Chapter Fourteen

No wonder she had never done great as a spy. Sure, Summer had gone through a few months of training before the DTRA had put her into an active intelligence-gathering role, but when it came to Mike, he had unmatched skills in actually listening to her and picking her reality apart. Whenever she was around him, it was as if he stripped her naked and exposed her in a way that only he could see.

That inability to conceal anything from him for very long, and the desire to not want to hide any of her truths, had to mean something about them was unique, unprecedented and whispering of soul mates. Didn't it?

She chuffed at the thought. No, that's not what was going on here. This was all because she had been forced to bring him into her little world and reveal more than she had anticipated. Though she hadn't meant to give him breadcrumbs that led him to the truth, that was exactly what she had done. There was nothing ethereal or otherworldly about their bond, no. It had all been set up by her subconscious mind.

She had wanted him to know the truth, to pull it from her. And more, to care.

Was her taking him down this path her subconscious way of making sure that if he was going to be in their lives, he would be willing to work for it?

Gah... She had to stop picking this thing between them apart. They just needed to work together, find Joe, and then they could figure things out between them.

Pulling over at a gas station, Summer watched as Mike got out to begin filling up her car. "I'm gonna go make a phone call. I'll be right back," she said.

Mike answered with a tight nod. He definitely hated Ben, and she didn't blame him, but this phone call had been his idea and he could hardly be annoyed that she was doing as he had asked.

The justification for her actions did little to stop the pull at her gut that told her to hide what she was doing to protect his feelings. And yet, at the same time, she didn't want to hide, she wanted him to know and to be a part of everything.

This was all so confusing. It had to be the stress that was messing her up like this. Just the stress.

She walked to the side of the building, far enough from the gas station's car wash that she didn't pick up too much background noise, and far enough from the entrance that anyone coming and going from the little convenience store couldn't eavesdrop.

As she was about to speed-dial Ben, she stopped and hit the number just two down from it on her Contacts list. Kevin answered on the first ring. "Hey, how's it going?"

"Hi, Kev. It's going. Any word on Joe?" She silently begged for a miracle.

"Were your ears burning?" he asked, a smattering of excitement in his voice.

"What is that supposed to mean? Did you get him back?"

Kevin sighed. "You and I both have chatted about this and you know that it is the US government's policy not to negotiate with terrorists. In this case, that terrorist is your son's kidnapper. However, I have finally gotten the approvals required from top brass to *assist* in your son's safe and rapid return."

Ah, the power that came with knowing the right people to call.

She rose on her tiptoes and put her free hand up against the beige stucco wall of the store. "Thank you... Kevin...thank you." Relief flooded through her, though she hadn't even heard Kevin's idea. No matter what he said, it had to be better than going to Ben and possibly tipping their hand to whomever else Ben was working with. As much as she had gone to bat for the man with Mike, she still didn't truly trust Ben. Not in her world of spies and counterspies.

"Don't thank me just yet, Summer," Kevin said, his voice suddenly taking on a serious edge. "First, we don't know if this is going to work, but it is what my team believes is the best option in this situation."

"And what is that? What are you guys thinking?"

She looked down at the dirt on the toes of her black boots.

"We have taken the code that you supplied us with from ConFlux and have altered it enough that it looks legitimate even to a proficient coder. Then we added in a few little lines here and there, which should help us pin down the IP address of whomever is trying to use it. Basically, once they run the program, we can swoop down and take these guys into custody."

"How long will it take you to get the code ready?" The kidnappers had only given her another twenty-four hours. The people at the DTRA would have to work fast.

"Well, this is the part you are really going to like. We are already done. We've been working on it ever since you told me about their demands."

"Kevin, you are amazing. No matter what the rest of the guys say."

"What? What are they saying?" Kevin said, laughter marking his words. "I will send you the code now through our encrypted server. Let me know when you put it into the kidnapper's hands."

"Will do," she said, smiling.

"And, Summer, give Joe a big hug from me." Kevin hung up.

She may possibly have the best boss ever. It took a special person to put his neck on the line to do what was right and go the extra mile to support his teams. And yet there was the little voice in the back of her head that screamed it was Kevin and her work as an agent within the DTRA that had really gotten her into this predicament.

Mike was just clicking the gas cap into place on her car when she made her way back out to the bay. "I have good news," she said, smiling over at him as she lifted her phone for him to see.

"Ben choked?" he joked.

"Better. I just got off the phone with my boss." She glanced around, looking for anyone or anything that was out of place. She motioned toward her car in the hope that if there was anyone following them or listening, she could thwart their attempts. "They have agreed to supply the fake code we need for the ransom. You are a smart guy with the idea for the code. Thanks to you and Kevin, we're going to get Joe back."

Mike flashed a smile but it was suddenly overtaken by a sour look.

Even to her own ears, the plan sounded simple... too simple. What was she missing?

"You know, kidnappers often kill—"

She cut him off with a raise of her hand. "I don't need to hear that. We don't even need to *think* about that happening to Joe. These people know the only chance they have to get the information they want is to give him to us. There would be no advantage in killing our son."

Mike nodded, but the look on his face didn't recede. "I just think we need to be prepared."

"There is being prepared and there is putting crap out into the universe that doesn't need to be put out into the universe." She was aware she sounded paranoid, but more times than she could count, when people put energy behind something, it tended to happen.

Losing Joe wasn't something she wanted to even imagine. Right now, they were just watching him... they would give him back. All she and Mike had to do was give them the information they wanted in exchange.

He put his hands up in surrender. "I hear what you are saying and I get it, but know that no matter what happens, I will be here for you."

She couldn't help but notice that for a split second Mike made it sound like Joe wasn't just as important to him as he was to her. Opening her mouth to argue, he stopped her with a glance.

"I know what you're going to say and you don't need to say it. If something happens to Joe, you know it will hurt me just as much as it may hurt you." His eyes shone. "I never thought I could instantly love anything or anyone like I love him. I know I've missed so much. And I wish I could have been there for all the milestones that I have already missed with him..." He hesitated, like he was attempting to collect himself, and it pulled at her heartstrings.

It was reassuring that he was just as invested. Though she hadn't been sure things would go this way when she had gone to see Mike, she was glad that he had so quickly embraced fatherhood. He had exceeded her expectations in his ability to be open and kind, generous of spirit and soul.

Since he'd left her at the altar, all she had done was focus on all the mistakes he had made in their relationship. She'd focused on the times he'd forgotten to text her back and had said the wrong things at dinner parties. She had spent all of her energy trying to stoke the fire that would burn away the love she had for him, and yet there standing with him, she was reminded that all it took was one spark to start a wildfire of passion. And damn, did this man know how to set her entire being ablaze.

"Nothing is going to happen to Joe," she said, choking on all the emotions that filled her.

"You know it," he said, wrapping his arm over her shoulders and walking her to the passenger side of the car. "Why don't you let me drive? Then you can work on getting the handoff scheduled."

She clicked on her seat belt as she waited for Mike to walk around and get into the driver seat. It was like the old days. They had slipped back into their habits so rapidly, and as much as she wanted to be annoyed—she had changed so much since they had been apart—she found solace in the familiar.

They had gotten answers. They were going to get Joe back, and yet she wasn't excited. If anything, she was terrified. What if something went wrong? What if Kevin didn't get her the information like he promised? What if the kidnappers didn't show?

She hated to get her hopes up.

She stared down at her phone, wondering what she should do next. Kevin was working on sending her the information she needed. There was only one thing she needed to do to get the ball rolling. She opened up her message app and tapped out a note to the number the kidnappers had used to contact them.

I have the code. Meet us at the Roadhouse. Half hour.

She waited for a reply as Mike fired up the engine and drove out of the bay and toward the road. He turned in the direction of her apartment, and she wanted to tell him not to, to go anywhere that would potentially lead them toward Joe, and yet she remained quiet. Just because they were driving, moving, it didn't mean they were moving in the correct direction.

Her phone's screen turned off.

What was taking them so long to get back to her?

Finally, after what seemed like an eternity, her phone beeped with a message.

They would meet them there in an hour, Joe in hand.

All they had to do was not screw this up. Get the code to the people, get Joe, and get out.

Doable. Very doable.

She raised her phone so that Mike could see the message. "The Roadhouse is only twenty minutes from here." She pointed for him to take the next left, leading them in the direction of the restaurant.

Mike smiled as he glanced over at the phone screen. "Good job."

She'd half expected him to say "here's hoping," but was glad when he didn't and instead let the air go still between them.

They rode in silence, the road noise filling the car. Her mind wandered to the restaurant, the layout. If they sat near the door, they would be in full view of everyone in the place. With witnesses came some level of additional safety. They could get Joe, get out.

Her phone pinged with a message from Kevin. The file was now in her hands and, with it, some of her fear lifted, just barely. So many things could go wrong, but she had to focus on getting everything just right.

The restaurant's parking lot was mostly full, but they found a spot not too far from the door. Her breath caught in her throat as she watched people walking in and out of the place, some getting in their cars while others chatted with friends before saying goodbye. Life was happening all around them.

No one knew about the terror and fear she had been feeling, only Mike. Was he feeling the same pressure, the clenching feeling, like everything in her future—and in Joe's—depended on this single meeting?

There was so much at stake, one wrong word or careless action could lead to her son's death, not to mention her own. Her life was of no consequence— she had chosen to put herself at risk thanks to her job—but Joe was innocent in all of this.

"Kevin sent the code," she said, forcing herself to focus on her phone in preparation for what she hoped would happen.

"If something goes wrong, and things come to guns, I want you to promise me that you will do everything you can to just get the hell out of there. I will take care of Joe—"

"I promise to get out of there, but only after I get Joe. I'm not letting him out of my sight ever again."

Mike smiled. "College is going to be really uncomfortable for him then."

She let out a laugh, the sound too sharp for the moment. "Think of all the things that I could save him from by always being there," she said, forcing a smile.

"He would be a chaste forty-year-old with a mommy complex for sure."

She laughed. "Oh, when you put it like that..."

Mike stepped out of the car, walked around and opened the door for her. He put out his hand. "Normal, happy couple. In and out. In ten minutes, Joe will be back in your arms and everything will be okay."

She smiled at the thought as she slipped her hand into Mike's. His hand was strong, just like the man.

This would all be okay.

Making their way inside, they chose a seat near the door so they could have full view of everyone who came and went from the restaurant. The eatery was busy, and the sounds of people talking and the smells of food cooking comforted her with their reminders of normalcy.

He took a seat next to her, sliding into the vinyl booth seat like they were out at just another dinner. Yes, she just had to fake it. Put a smile on her face and act like they weren't giving false information to a terrorist group to get an infant back from kidnappers.

Just another day. No big deal.

How had her life gotten to this point? At what moment had things taken this dark turn? And how could she avoid ever finding herself back in a moment like this?

She picked up a menu after a server brought them their drinks. She stared at the pictures of food and the letters that she knew spelled words, but she wasn't reading. All she could think about was how her hands were trembling and how she had to force them to stay as still as possible so as to not raise any sort of suspicion.

The front door of the restaurant opened and two men came in. In their arms was Joe's gray car seat.

What if they were playing a trick on her? What if Mike was right and they had hurt Joe?

Until now, she had thought waiting for the men and counting down the seconds until they arrived was the worst part. But now she was sure it was this moment that was the most painful. Being close enough to her son to almost see his smiling face and yet far enough away that he could be gone in an instant made her feel as if she was staring into an abyss.

The man closest to them looked over, spotted them and said something to the man carrying the baby. Their faces were tight and, as the second man looked over at them, a dark cloud rolled across his features. They walked like they were half dead with exhaustion.

They trudged toward them and, as they moved, she could make out the unmistakable bulges of guns tucked into the waistbands of their pants near their appendixes. Her throat tightened. She and Mike weren't the only ones ready and willing to fight.

Mike reached down, under the edge of the table, and put his hand on her knee like some kind of steadying force to remind her that everything was okay. "We got this," he said under his breath.

She didn't dare look away from the men approaching their table, but she answered Mike with a slight nod. One way or another, they were going to do this thing. Here was hoping that the three of them made it out of this alive and the two men who had dared to steal their baby would end up paying for their actions.

"Evening," the man carrying the car seat said, but there was only falseness in his tone.

He and his friend slipped into the booth as a hostess brought over an antiquated wooden high chair and helped them set the car seat up at the end of the table. Summer stared at the car seat as the hostess lifted it into view, but she could only see the gray polka-dotted coverlet she used when Joe was sleeping.

"Thank you," she said, dipping her head toward the hostess as she turned to leave.

The woman smiled at her like she was just another customer on just another day.

Summer wrapped her foot around the base of the high chair and pulled the wooden stand closer to her.

"Hold up," the man across the table said, grabbing the high chair and stopping Summer from moving it any closer to her.

"Look, it's not like I'm going to pick Joe up and just go running out of here. We have a deal, but before I agree to anything, I have to know that my baby is all right." She scowled.

The man raised his hands in surrender, letting her pull the high chair over to her. "Just know that if you screw with us, we will hunt you down. Next time, we will kill the kid and you."

She could feel the blood rush from her features as she thought about the ruse she and her DTRA team were playing on the men, but she forced herself to focus on Joe.

She opened the coverlet. Joe was inside, his eyes closed and a pacifier in his mouth. The pacifier was the cheap plastic kind found at any big-box store, not the usual blue silicone ones that he preferred. Reaching in, she ran her thumb across Joe's warm cheek. As she touched his soft skin, he let out a contented sigh and his lips pulled into a smile, the pacifier teetering on his lower lip.

Joe was fine. The men had kept their promise and kept her and Mike's baby safe.

The heaviness that had filled Summer ever since Joe had disappeared started to lift. They were all going to be okay as long as they could make it out of this restaurant without a problem.

"You've seen him," the man said, pulling the high

chair away from her and forcing her hand from her baby. "Now, you need to give us the code."

"Look, I'm his mother, and I need to hold him. You can take those guns you're carrying and shoot us all, but then you won't get the code, and you probably won't make it out of here alive—or you don't know Montana."

"If you think you can touch that baby without first giving us what we are here for, then you don't value his life. You really think it's worth taking the risk?" the man asked, arching a brow.

She reached down and grabbed her phone, but she didn't take her gaze off of Joe. He looked so peaceful, so blithely unaware of the drama that had surrounded him and brought him to this moment.

"Before she gives you anything, we need to make sure you know that once we give it to you, that's it," Mike said. "We are out. No more harassing us or putting your hands on Joe. If you touch him again, I will kill you. Got it?" He put his hand on hers before she had a chance to activate her phone to retrieve the information.

The man who had been carrying Joe chortled. "Man, if you think we want to babysit ever again, you are bat shit crazy." As the man peered over at them, she could make out the dark circles under his eyes, which were normally indicative of a new parent, or in this case, an underprepared kidnapper. "But first we gotta get what we came here for."

Whatever Joe had put them through, these jerks had had it coming.

Noticing the tiredness in their features, a sense of vindication filled her. At least Joe hadn't made it easy on them.

Good job, baby. She smiled in Joe's direction. Hopefully he would never lose that fighting spirit. Well, unless she was the one fighting him. Then she prayed he would take it just a little easy on her.

The man nearest the wall pulled out a small tablet she hadn't noticed him carrying and brushed aside a few crumbs the busser had neglected to wipe away.

"Rico here is going to check your code. If something is up, if it doesn't look exactly like it should, then we will kill the baby." The man nearest to Joe pointed at the car seat. "And believe me, we will be more than happy to do it. That little bastard kept us up all night and we haven't eaten in over twenty-four hours. I'm tired, I'm hungry, and I'm pissed... so don't screw with us."

No matter how uncomfortable and pissed off these guys were, it paled in comparison to everything they had put her through. If he thought he was scaring her, that he had any power over her now that Joe was so close, he was wrong. All she cared about was that baby.

But then, she wasn't going to get out of here if Kevin had screwed her on this. And Kevin and the DTRA had already made a mistake in failing to understand or to foresee the consequences in her data breach and theft. If they'd had their acts together, she, Mike and Joe wouldn't be in the position in which they now found themselves.

Could she really trust that Kevin had done everything in his power to make things right? Or had he and his IT team just phoned it in?

"Where do you want me to send the code?" she said, careful to keep her voice down.

The man pushed a slip of paper across the table with an email address. "Send it here."

She opened up her phone and clicked on the file Kevin had sent her. With a few more presses of buttons, the file was in cyber space and moving toward the kidnappers. "You should have it."

Her heart thrashed in her chest. This was the moment. The moment everything could go wrong. The moment Joe could be hurt, and it would all be her fault.

Had she been wrong to trust? Had she been wrong to come here? Had she been wrong to think that agreeing to lie to her enemy was the best course of action?

The man tapped a few keys on his tablet as Rico watched over his shoulder. They looked like two nervous schoolboys, which made her wonder exactly how high up in the ranks they were. Based on their fumbling of the kidnapping and this, it was easy to tell these two men were nothing more than the instruments of someone else's will…someone who didn't want their name or face to be known. The thought helped ease some of the tension Summer was feeling.

Hopefully these two didn't know good code from bad.

The man looking over the code turned to Rico and gave him a stiff nod, seemingly pleased with the information she had forwarded.

Without another word, the man slid out of the booth and stood. Rico gave her a vicious smile. "Here's hoping we never have to see you again. If we do, you and everyone you know will wind up dead."

Chapter Fifteen

To say things had gone unexpectedly was a bit of an understatement. In his wildest dreams, Mike would not have imagined that he and Summer would simply get Joe and be on their merry way within minutes. They had been fighting this so hard, and struggling to find workarounds, that the answer and the hand-off just seemed far too simple.

He didn't trust it.

Nothing of value was ever that easy. Especially not when it came to the safety of the people he cared about most.

Arriving back at Summer's apartment, he helped her bring Joe inside. Neither had said more than five words to each other since they had left the restaurant. From the worried expression on Summer's face, he wondered if she was feeling the same way. It surprised him that she had wanted to come back to her apartment at all. If he had been in her shoes, he would've bugged out and found himself on the next plane to South America.

She carried Joe in his car seat to her bedroom

and he could hear her unclipping the seat belt and Joe gurgling as she must have lifted him out. She hummed as she set about working. Mike walked down the hall, stopping at her bedroom door and peering inside.

Joe was lying on the bed, kicking his feet in the air as he blissfully watched his mother take a suitcase down from her closet. After it was down, she grabbed a diaper to change her son, but Mike stepped in to take over.

"Thanks," she said. "He is acting pretty good, but I want him to be clean and dry when I hit the road."

So, she was planning on leaving. And Mike couldn't ignore the fact that she had only said *I*. Did that mean she had no intention of taking Joe with her, or was she planning on taking Joe but not him?

"Where do you think you are going to go?" Mike asked.

"If those guys are smart," she said with a dark laugh, "then by now they probably know that something is up with the code."

She hadn't answered his question.

"Do you really think they figured out it was bad code that fast?" He took the diaper she held, along with the bucket of baby wipes and the mat.

He glanced at Joe. They exchanged a look with one another like each knew exactly how poorly this diaper change was about to go. While he had changed a diaper in the past, it had been at least twenty years ago when he'd taken home a lifelike doll from his health class and put it through the ringer. And while the requirements for a good diaper change were probably the same, he wasn't sure whether diapers were or not. In fact, he couldn't remember or not if he actually used duct tape last time he'd been asked to do this.

"Rico and the other dude may not have figured it out, but whomever they are working for probably has…or is probably about to. All they have to do is run it on a big enough server and they are going to encounter errors."

"You are assuming the information they are looking for isn't buried deep." As much as he thought he understood IT and cyber security, he still felt out of his depths. "What exactly was the coding used for?"

"IGS," she snapped.

"That, I'm more than aware of. I know it's for the information gathering systems." How could he forget a bug that could infiltrate anyone's home and life? "I guess what I'm asking is why they couldn't just write this code themselves, or find someone who could?" he pressed, hoping for a real answer this time.

"Does it matter?" She raised her arms akimbo, giving him that cute look that used to make him forget what he was doing and sent them straight to the bed…the bed that was now hosting a wiggly baby.

Joe made a little raspberry sound as he stuffed the back of his fist into his wet mouth.

"Even you know she's being ridiculous, don't you, little guy?"

Joe kicked his feet as Mike went about stripping him down, making getting his little doll-size clothes off something closer to a rodeo event than the bliss-ful moments he'd seen on television commercials.

"You want to put the extra diaper under his bum, and get a wipe ready for the splash zone." She mo-tioned at her undercarriage.

Yep, this was definitely something he could imag-ine at the annual Arlee Rodeo. He could almost imagine the announcer talking through the tinny ring of an outdated sound system, his words coming faster and faster as he neared the eight-second mark.

He pulled out a wipe after slipping the clean, open diaper under Joe. Joe tried to roll, forcing Mike to hold him in place with one hand while trying to close the open lid of the container with the other. Appar-ently, juggling was also part of this rodeo act; and… well, he was quickly starting to feel as if he was play-ing the clown.

Summer put down a shirt that she was folding and stepped forward as if she was going to take over the operation.

"Nope," he said, putting his hand up to stop her. "You do your thing. Joe and I've got this." He smiled down at Joe. "If we are going to be buddies, then I'm going to have to figure this dad thing out."

Summer turned away from them, but not before he saw a pained expression flash across her face. She had brought him here and into their lives with all kinds of talk about him taking on an active role as Joe's father. But now that things were getting a bit more complicated, it felt like she was driving a wedge between them.

What else was there to say? What could he do to reassure her and make her see that he was going to be in their lives, and protecting them as long as he needed to?

"I know you're scared right now, but I told you before that I got you. If I need to get STEALTH on board for security or whatever...we can do it. We specialize in helping people in situations all too much like this."

She didn't turn to face him, just waved her hand in acknowledgment.

He opened Joe's sodden diaper and set about changing him, moving as rapidly as he could to keep from getting the mess anywhere it shouldn't be. Joe looked up at him with wide eyes, his lower lip starting to quiver as he grew chilled.

He let out a long wail, followed by a stream of warm liquid...hitting Mike's center mass. "Oh! Oh crap..." he said, covering Joe up with the clean diaper as fast as his hands would allow. Joe stopped wailing as Mike fastened the last strip over the baby's waist and slipped his pants back on over his flailing legs. Picking him up, he held him in one arm.

Joe's wail stopped and he went back to sucking on the back of his hand as Mike looked down at his soaked shirt.

The damage was done.

From beside him, Summer's laughter rang through the air. "I told you to watch out for the splash zone!" she said between laughs.

"A little splash zone I can deal with, but this—"

he motioned toward his shirt "—was like sitting front row on Splash Mountain."

"No one said you weren't going to get your hands dirty," she teased. "I offered to take over, but no… someone was trying to be all cute and charming with his little fatherly act."

Mike wasn't sure if he should be offended or bemused, so he went with the latter. "Cute, huh? You think me getting peed on is cute?" He picked up the sodden diaper and wrapped it into a little ball.

"Don't you dare throw that at me, if you do…"

"What?" he taunted, holding it up a little higher in a mock threat. "What would you do to me?"

She stepped closer to him and they stood chest to chest, with her looking up at him. "You think you are real tough, don't you?" There was a look in her eyes that made him temporarily forget everything other than her and the boy in his arms.

That look. He loved that look; he had seen a flash of it last night. But this time it was different. This time it didn't carry the pain of the past; instead it only spoke of the present and begged for a future.

"I'm always stronger when I'm with you," he whispered into her hair after leaning in.

She melded into him, Joe between them as she wrapped her arms around Mike and he took her with his free hand. This. This was his family. No matter if they were married or not married, in a relationship or not. These were the people he would happily lay down his life to protect and love.

There was nothing he wouldn't do for them.

"Babe, I hope you know how much I love you." The pressure that had been building in his chest from the first moment he had seen her in the parking lot released as he spoke the words.

There was a long silence. The only sound was of Joe making smacking noises as he sucked on his hand.

Summer didn't have to say anything back. He didn't care. He just couldn't hold those words in any longer. Not when they had already gone through so much, and not with her leaving without him.

She needed to know the truth—that his love for her hadn't gone anywhere and hadn't diminished with time. His love for her would be with him until his dying day, no matter the status of their relationship.

There was a bang on the apartment's front door and Summer jerked out of his arms. "What the hell?" Her voice sounded strangled by fear. "You don't think Rockwood found us already, do you?"

That was fast, but so was everything else in their lives.

"It's going to be okay," he said, handing her Joe. "You just take him and go into the bathroom. Get into the tub in case things move to guns. No matter what happens, I will deal with it."

"You can't go out there alone." She pulled Joe against her body, wrapping her arms around him like she was his shield.

"And we can't risk Joe getting hurt or taken again.

If they get their hands on any of us, I have a feeling we aren't going to make it out of this alive."

Her eyes widened as his words struck home. "You…you have to be careful."

There was another series of bangs on the door, the sound reverberating through the apartment like church bells beckoning from their tower.

He nodded, motioning her to hide in the small en suite bathroom. "Go."

Watching to make sure the door clicked closed behind her, Mike made his way out of the bedroom and into the living room. He stared at the white door for a long moment. If he looked out through the peephole, he was the perfect target for anyone standing on the other side just waiting for the right moment to pull a trigger.

If there was a suppressor on the weapon, no one in the apartment complex would even know what was happening. The attackers could shoot him, come in and kill Joe and take Summer. Or, they could kill them all.

Summer was strong, capable, smart, and myriad wonderful things, but he was more practiced and physically stronger and, right now, he was their first line of defense. He couldn't just let an attacker get a bead on him, not when so many lives were at stake.

He rushed to the back door, silently closing and locking it as he slipped outside. The night air had the bite of coming frost and carried with it the unmistakable odor of danger.

The alley behind the apartment building was

empty and he was careful to step lightly as he made his way down the potholed road and around the side of the building. Thankfully all the apartment blinds were closed. He made sure to remain concealed as he glanced around the side of the building. Standing in front of her door was a man, late fifties, gray hair, and he was wearing a suit jacket.

Though the man didn't look like either of the men who had taken Joe, Mike couldn't be sure that he wasn't their boss or someone else from the Rockwood organization. If anything, it was smart to send someone they didn't recognize, someone who could get in and get out without really being noticed.

Then again, if this guy was going for being unnoticed, what was he doing banging on the door? If the man was like Mike, he would have slipped in through the back of the apartment, done what needed to be done, and then slipped out into the darkness of the night.

Their murders would have gone unsolved forever.

It struck Mike how wrong it was that he was, in fact, planning their deaths.

He was warped. Yet it was this ability to think about the unthinkable and to plan for the worst that had made him effective as a military contractor. Death was inevitable; it was just how one got there that was up for grabs. And today, he would be pushing it away with both hands and maybe a foot to the ass.

The man banged on the door again, looking over his shoulder as if he could feel Mike watching him in the moonlight. It was odd how the human being had a sixth sense when it came to danger and yet rarely actually listened to it.

Yes, the man was right to be afraid. If he was smart, he should have listened to the fear and turned tail and gone back to where he had come from.

Tonight, he was playing with fire.

The man shifted slightly, his back to Mike as he looked out toward the main road. Mike slipped around the side of the building as he unholstered his gun and stalked forward. The man had pulled his phone out of his back pocket and was hitting buttons as Mike drew nearer.

He was so close that he could smell the man's expensive cologne and make out the faint red line on the back of the man's neck where he must have recently gotten a haircut. The guy put the phone up to his ear. "She's not here. Are you sure this is where you tracked her phone to?"

Oh crap.

Mike wished he could hear what the other person was saying, but all he could catch was a guttural moan escaping the man's throat. "I'm sure that she is going to go underground, given what happened to her son. We've trained her well enough."

Was this someone from the DTRA? Was her team swooping in to help her out? Something about the man's being there, even if he was someone from the DTRA, didn't quite sit right with Mike. Why wouldn't they have told Summer that they were coming? Why would they just roll up on her door in the middle of the night, especially knowing all that she had recently gone through?

"We need to get a bead on her. Use your resources," the man said, clicking off his phone and stuffing it back into his pocket.

The man moved as if about to turn around, but before he could, Mike grabbed him by the neck, effectively pinning his head in a choke hold as he pushed his Glock's cold steel barrel against the guy's temple. "Who the hell are you? And what the hell are you doing here?"

The man gave a slight yelp, moving for what Mike was sure was a weapon at his waist.

He pressed the Glock harder against the man's temple, no doubt leaving a nice little ring on his flesh. "That's a bad idea. Just tell me who you are."

"My name's Kevin. Kevin Warble. I work with Summer. I'm here to help." The man spoke fast, brusquely.

"Help her with what?" Mike could give the man nothing, no clues he had any idea about what was going on or why.

"She is in danger. I can't tell you anything else." Kevin looked at him as Mike tightened his hold around the man's neck.

"Did they use the code? Are they coming for her?" Mike asked, giving the guy just enough information to make it clear that he wasn't completely in the dark.

Kevin said nothing but scowled and then moved to break out. Mike pulled tighter. "Dude, I don't want to hurt you. I just need to get some damned answers.

Why are you making this harder on yourself than it needs to be?"

The man sighed. "I wasn't expecting Summer to have a security detail."

"You thought you could just come here and get the drop on her?" Mike countered.

"What?" Kevin stopped moving. "Why in the hell would I want to hurt Summer? She is a tremendous asset to our team."

Mike kept his gun firmly pointed at the man's head as he let go of his neck and allowed him to stand straight. "You can't expect me to believe you are standing out here and banging on her door in the middle of the night for her own good. So why are you here? Are they coming for her?" he asked again.

"We have reason to believe so, yes. They ran the code." Kevin scowled. "I have to admit I'm disappointed you have any knowledge of what is happening here."

"Well, if you hadn't left Summer with her ass hanging out then maybe she wouldn't have had to come to me for help. If you are pissed, you need to look to yourself. As you said, Summer is a tremendous member of your team, and she has always been the same to me."

Kevin glanced away, like he, too, had known the DTRA had made a mistake when it came to the safety of one of their team members. "It wasn't our intention for anything to happen as it has. We didn't believe Rockwood had any knowledge as to what she had gained access to and had managed to send to us.

If we had, you have to know we would have done everything in our power to keep her safe."

"You should have gotten out in front of this," Mike said.

"And you should lower that gun, but it seems like we are both a little bit jumpy when it comes to this situation."

This situation? The man talked about Summer's life like it was an afterthought. No wonder she had run to Mike for help.

He didn't like this man, not at all. But he lowered his weapon. For now, the only person who could find a way out of this muddied circumstance was the one person who Mike wanted to keep safe.

Hopefully he wasn't making a mistake in letting this man come close to the woman he loved.

Chapter Sixteen

Summer stared at Kevin like he had lost his mind. "You want me to do what?" she repeated.

Kevin smiled, the action saturated with remorse. "Your friend, Mike, was right in what he said out there. It was wrong of us to put you in this kind of situation. And I know that this solution is the best. It will keep you out of the line of fire for a while."

They stood in her living room, arguing. As soon as Mike had let Kevin in, he'd started to explain his plan. It was simple, straightforward, and unattractive. Be carted off to a safe spot. Alone.

"And what about Joe and Mike? Do you really expect me to just pack my bags and disappear? Leave my child behind?" She looked over at Mike. She didn't want to leave him; he seemed like the only person in her life who really had her best interests and her safety in mind. And she couldn't bear the thought of leaving Joe, who now slept peacefully in his crib in the back bedroom.

"I know that you are probably thinking this sounds crazy, but you need to keep your son safe.

Mike can take him until we get a hold on these Rockwood people and can guarantee your safety. Then you can come back." Kevin paused. "You knew when you took this job that things weren't always going to be ideal when it came to having this career and a child. I'm sorry, but now it is time to follow through on your oath."

Her entire body clenched with resentment and anger. She had fallen into the "it won't happen to me" trap when she'd agreed to work for the DTRA. She had told herself that she was putting Joe first by taking the job with its financial security and eventual stability. She would only be a field agent for a short period of time and yet, here she was, paying the reaper for her hubris in thinking she had the world on a string.

It seemed like she would never be able to do the right thing.

She had promised that she wouldn't leave Joe again and here she was…

If she took Joe with her, he would be in danger—even on a military base. And what would she do with him while she went to work? They wouldn't let her take him into the field office, and she'd be damned if she'd leave him in the hands of a stranger. So that left her at odds again. Mike was her only option, but it still meant leaving Joe.

"Your son will be safer not being with you until we get this sorted. If you want, I can have him placed in a foster home if you don't feel good leaving him alone with him." Kevin motioned toward Mike.

"Oh hell no." She shook her head violently, nauseated by the mere thought of someone she didn't even know having physical custody of her baby after she had just gotten him back to safety. "Mike can take him. I will go with you."

"Perfect," Kevin said, his remorseful smile growing. "We have a private plane waiting on the tarmac just outside the air base. They will take us to Kirtland Air Force Base in New Mexico. You can hole up while we gain control over the situation."

Summer couldn't believe that this was what it had come down to: to save the people she loved, she had to leave them alone.

"Don't worry," Mike said, reaching over and touching her on the shoulder like she was nothing more than a friend. "I will take great care of Joe. If I need any help, I can always turn to Jess. You don't need to worry about us, you just need to get to a safe location before something else happens."

She just couldn't wrap her mind around this. She had made a promise to herself that she wouldn't leave Joe again; not when there were people out there who were willing and able to get their hands on him and put him in the ground to get to her.

Why did she have to make the choice between two men who had promised her the world, one out of love and the other with her career—but both central to her past, present and future? Mike had hurt her, deeply. Yet, there was no doubt in her mind that she could trust him with Joe. There were no safer hands.

Kevin's phone pinged with some kind of message.

"I'll be right back," he said, turning away from them and stepping outside to answer.

"Are you really sure you can trust this man?" Mike murmured quietly, a look of total disgust marring his handsome face.

"Why do you ask?" Summer didn't want to tell Mike she didn't know if she could or she couldn't; she didn't know what to do or what the right answer was.

"Everything about him makes me want to tell you to run. I can keep you safe. I can keep both you and Joe safe."

"I have a feeling that you would say that about any man I have in my life. Ben as evidence."

He wrinkled his nose. "I don't like Ben and I don't like Kevin. And to my credit, I ended up being right about Ben." He gave her a long, studying look. "What are you not telling me about Kevin?"

There were many things she could have told Mike about Kevin, from how he took his coffee to how he had an odd penchant for liking to use Helvetica font in his emails. On the variety of field exercises and cases she had worked with him, she had started to pick up on some of his quirks. When he was nervous, Kevin always tapped his fingertips on his left thigh. He was rarely nervous, but when he was, it normally led to more trouble than she could handle.

"What do you want to know?"

The door opened and Kevin strode back into the apartment. "Our plane got delayed. There are heavy winds coming out of the north. Winter storm warnings tonight, and they are projecting at least a foot of snow in the overnight hours. Looks like we won't be traveling anywhere. However, the pilot says he thinks we can get out midmorning tomorrow."

Summer let out a breath she hadn't realized she was holding. From the back room came the soft cries of Joe as he began to wake up. "I need to go take care of him. Just let me know what time you want me to meet up in the morning. In the meantime, I will make some arrangements for the night…anywhere but here."

Mike smirked. "Why don't you just go ahead and track her like you did earlier."

She twitched. "What are you talking about?"

"Your boss tracked you down thanks to your phone." Mike started to say something else but was cut off when Kevin moved between them.

"How else was I going to find you? You haven't been answering your phone. I needed to find you."

She felt violated. Sure, Kevin had the right and the permission to look into her whereabouts, but she couldn't remember actually ignoring any phone calls from him. Then again, she had been putting her phone in and out of the Faraday bag all day. Maybe she had missed some.

"I thought you were hurt. That Rockwood may have already gotten to you after the handoff," Kevin continued, "And I feel that it's absolutely ridiculous that I have to explain myself to you, Mike, or anyone else. You work for me."

Mike tried to say something, but Kevin shut him

down with a backhanded wave. "Before things get even more out of hand here, I am going to leave. If you need help finding accommodations for the night, or if you want me to get you additional security, all you have to do is let me know. We are here for you." He walked out without another look in Mike's direction, closing the door behind him with a thump.

Joe let out a piercing wail from the bedroom and Summer rushed out of the room. What was she going to do? Should she just hit the road with Joe and not look back? And what about Mike? Should she take him with them? Or should she follow the rules and honor the oaths she had made to her job? She could just quit and hand over everything she had been working on. There were plenty of people who could do what she could do.

But Kevin really did seem to care. Sure, her boss had made mistakes in his handling of this situation, but he had personally come down to see her. He had set up a private jet to fly them somewhere he felt she could be safe. He had offered to be her escort to safety.

And so had Mike.

She ran her hands over her face as she walked into the bedroom. Joe was sitting up in his crib, looking out at her as tears welled in his eyes. "Baby..." she cooed. "Did we wake you up, sweetheart? Mama is so sorry." She reached in and scooped him up into her arms, pressing his warm, pudgy body against her chest like he was her security blanket and not the other way around.

She wished she could get him to her pediatrician for a quick checkup just to make sure those thugs hadn't done anything to him when they'd had him. She'd have to figure out how to do that soon. He looked healthy and well-fed, though, and she hadn't seen a bruise or a scratch on him.

Humming "Two Little Blackbirds," she rocked back and forth taking comfort in these stolen moments of presumed safety. She pulled the rich odor of baby deep into her lungs. He smelled so good. She would never forget that smell and the feeling in her chest it created.

This little being…this was her world. What else really mattered?

Her thoughts moved to Mike, to the day he had left her standing at the altar. In that moment, he had chosen to keep her safe in the only way he'd known how—by leaving her. Now, all of a sudden, standing here with a similar choice to make, she finally understood the level of love and pain he had to have been feeling to have made such a devastating choice.

Until now, she had thought that his actions had been out of some misguided fear and paranoia; that he had walked away out of cowardice. More, when he had broken her heart, he had dishonored the promises he had made to her.

She had been wrong.

Though she didn't believe he could love her in the same way she loved Joe, Summer could understand what Mike must have been feeling…the conflicting need to honor or to protect.

In their lines of work, to have the ability to do both was idealistic. They lived in a world of "either-or" but never "and."

What she could have was this one night.

She looked down at Joe, who had drifted off to sleep. Ever so gently, she placed him back in his crib, covering him up with her favorite elephant blanket. If only she could feel as safe and as loved, but also have the ability to forget the fear when he had disappeared.

Turning from the crib, she found Mike standing in the doorway of the bedroom. "I could watch that every night for the rest of my life."

"I hate to tell you this, but Joe won't stay a baby forever." She smiled, taking pleasure in this simple moment of them acting as a family, though it was edged with the sadness that came with growing children.

"What if Joe wasn't our only baby?" he asked.

But he had to have been teasing.

She stayed quiet as she tiptoed out of the room, having him move behind her.

"I mean, how many kids do you think you would want, if you could…" Mike added.

Just when she thought her life couldn't get any more complicated, there he went throwing this kind of talk at her. But maybe Mike was trying to help her take her mind off the danger that could be lurking just outside.

"I thought we talked about this," she said with a tired smile. "I always wanted a boy and a girl. If that didn't happen, I would want to keep trying until I had both sexes."

"I know you said that, but you know that isn't really an answer. According to that answer, we could end up having a dozen boys and still be trying for a girl."

"We?" She couldn't help the smile that spread on her face. "Are you saying you want to have more kids with me?"

He shrugged, suddenly taken with looking at the floor. "When and if things between us are right, I mean."

"Are you saying that you want to start over?" she pressed, excitement coursing through her as she spoke. Mike wasn't the kind who had been overly talkative when it came to his feelings, his wants, or the future.

Sure, they'd had a few conversations, but it had been years since the last one like this.

He finally looked up. "Summer, I told you how sorry I am for what happened."

She stopped him as she nodded and took his hand in hers. "Don't worry. For the first time, I think I understand. Truly. I don't envy the choices you've had to make and I never want you to have to make them again. From here on out, let's just be honest with one another. If you are afraid, if you feel like running, then tell me. We can talk about it. If nothing else, we can run away together—as a family."

The fear that seemed to have permanently settled on his features lately lifted as he pulled her close.

"Babe, I have loved you forever. I *will* love you forever. Do you remember the first time we met?" he asked, levity in his voice.

She laughed at the memory. It had been in Las Vegas, at a George Strait concert. For once, it had been raining in the desert city and everyone lined up outside was being drenched by the dust-laden droplets. Jess had been there with her, their annual girl's trip to the city. They had spent hours getting ready, curling their hair and styling their eyebrows on point. And with each torrent, their hair flattened and their makeup smeared farther and farther down their faces. She could still remember how Jessica's mascara had run down so far that it had made a black streak on her neck.

When Mike had first walked up, with his brother AJ, she and Jessica had been laughing about the state of themselves and trying to hide under their purses to no avail.

"You have always thought of yourself as quite the hero, haven't you?" she teased, thinking about how Mike had produced—out of seemingly nowhere—two ponchos for the women.

"I was definitely your hero that day." He laughed. "Not to mention, your hero when we poured you into the cab later that night."

"Oh yeah…" She had forgotten that part.

In truth, she hadn't planned on ever seeing Mike and AJ after that, but Jess had, at some point in the night, given the guys their phone numbers.

"If you hadn't badgered me," she continued, "you know I wouldn't have gone out with you again."

He laughed. "Yeah, but I could tell in the way you professed your love to me that night that you were the girl I wanted to spend the rest of my life with."

Summer covered her face in embarrassment. "Not one of my proudest moments. I told you then, and I think it begs repeating, but you know I'm not usually that kind of girl. I never cut loose like I did that night. I just…"

"Felt safe?" he said, finishing her sentence.

She nodded.

"You will always be safe with me. I will never hurt you again. Ever."

That wasn't a promise anyone in the world could make and keep, but she appreciated the thought. It was enough to know he would always be her guardian, the keeper of her heart, and the father of her child.

Not to mention that she loved him. She loved him so, so much.

And yet she didn't have time for that right now… They had to get out of here and away from this choke point before Rockwood's people came knocking.

She looked up at him and gave him a gentle kiss on his cheek. "I love you, too, Mike. But I won't make a promise I know I can't keep." She pulled out of his arms and turned away before he could see any of the pain she knew had to be registering on her face. It would have been the perfect moment to tell him she promised him the world too, but perfection was an illusion.

She'd rather have something that was real—and something she could keep forever.

"Do you mind grabbing my bag? I can make a hotel reservation once we hit the road." She didn't look back at him. Not yet, she needed a moment to get control of herself.

Safety had to come first. Then they could talk all he wanted. In the morning, though, she would have to leave them…no matter what. With love came the responsibility to protect.

There was the creak of the bedroom door as he went for her things.

This was going to be their last night together, possibly forever. If something happened to her at Kirtland, this could be the last night she spent with Joe.

The thought made her feel as though her heart was being ripped from her chest.

How could she leave her son? But how could she justify putting him in harm's way just so that she could be a constant in his life?

From the very beginning of Mike's entrance back into their lives, she had told Mike he couldn't just come and go from Joe's life at the drop of a hat and according to his schedule. And yet she was doing exactly what she had told him not to. To say she felt like a hypocrite was a major understatement.

If she did get to see the boys again, there was no way she could ever draw lines in the sand. They would be equal…which maybe wasn't a bad thing.

She had wanted Mike to be a co-parent. Cooperation and compromise. And maybe, someday, something more.

Mike came out of the bedroom, her bag and the diaper bag in one arm and Joe cradled in the other, his sleeping face lying on his daddy's shoulder. A lump swelled in her throat at the wholesome sight; a sight she couldn't have imagined just a few months ago.

How fast and how dramatically life had a way of changing.

"If you grab the door, I will take everything outside." He looked her in the eyes. "And don't worry, this time I won't leave Joe alone. Not even for a second. We will meet you out there."

She answered with a dip of her head. "Just wait, let's go together," she said, opening the front door for them.

The apartment complex was quiet, but its peace was merely an illusion. Kevin and his team may well have been perched outside, watching and keeping guard. And on their heels could have been the Rockwood crew.

Would she ever really feel safe again?

Mike had his head on a swivel as he stepped out the door. She looked back, around her apartment. This was probably the last time she would be here. There wasn't much, a chair and a few boxes, and she wouldn't miss any of her things; but she would miss having a home.

Someday, maybe she would have stability in her life again. Until then, she'd say goodbye.

Chapter Seventeen

The snow had started to fall, coating the world in a silent blanket as they arrived at the hotel. After checking them in under a false name and acting like a happy little family of three, Mike got Joe and Summer into their room and then moved the car. He parked it two miles away, in front of another hotel, making sure to leave Summer's phone inside the glovebox, should anyone try to track her down again.

He expected they had been followed by Summer's people at the DTRA. That was exactly what he would have done—have a shadow surveillance team securing the perimeter at all times. If they didn't, and something happened, it would be even more of a black eye for the agency when they had to write up the reports. Congress would have a field day if they found out a baby had been put in danger, especially when it came time to allot funding for the program.

If Kevin was smart, he would be on his toes making sure that no further harm came to them.

Here was hoping. It was naive and idiotic to assume anyone was going to protect them. It was like the law enforcement adage about rural areas: "we aren't your first line of defense, we are merely the report takers after the fact."

More times than not, he had seen that sentiment in action. And he would be damned if he was going to be complacent and fall for the dupe of assumed safety.

Walking back to the hotel, he let the snowflakes land on his face. The chill felt good on his skin, invigorating. He had only been in Montana for less than a year; it had been a long time since he had been a part of a true winter. It was no secret that the place could be brutal, winds up to a hundred miles an hour sending snow sideways, blinding and freezing the world as it tore through the countryside.

If that was what they were in for tonight, it was no wonder the pilot had put a stop to them flying out. Truth be told, Mike was thankful she had been forced to stay for one more night. It was greedy and more than dangerous to keep Summer here, with her enemies possibly on the hunt for her, but he wanted as much time with her as he could get.

He quickened his pace, jogging toward the hotel as he carefully picked his way around icy patches on the sidewalks and the ever-growing snowdrifts starting to build alongside the road.

By the time he got back, he was breathing hard and the light layer of sweat that had started to accumulate on his skin just as quickly evaporated into the dry winter air. The blast of warmth hit him like a freight train as he entered the hotel lobby. The man behind the registration desk looked up and, recognizing him, sent him an acknowledging tip of the head.

Ah, small towns. They were part of the world in which only a few things, things in the darkness of the night, went unnoticed or, at least, unspoken.

He hadn't missed that aspect of Montana. He had always loved the anonymity that came with being a member of STEALTH. But tonight, for once, he was just a man…at least as far as the people in this hotel needed to know. He didn't need them being suspicious if he acted outside of the norm. For now, the best thing he could do was to merely blend in and hope he had a forgettable face.

He tapped on their hotel room door before making his way inside. Joe must have been in the travel crib; a blanket was draped over the bars. Summer was perched on the bed, her knees up, as she watched some kind of true crime television show on the flat-screen.

She put her fingers to her lips as he walked in, then pointed at the crib, motioning that Joe was asleep.

There were so many things he wanted to talk to her about and so many questions that he wanted to ask—about what plans she had in mind, and how they would keep in touch when she went away. When Kevin had requested he take Joe, Mike's first reaction had been absolute and abject fear. He was in no way capable of taking care of a baby alone. The kid had peed on him; he could only imagine what else was in store. He didn't know much about taking care of a baby, and if he didn't have Summer standing over his shoulder and coaching him along, Mike wasn't sure he would really know what to do.

That being said, he would be more than happy to take his son. It was his duty as the father and, even if he wasn't Joe's dad, he would have done it for her.

Summer sat up and moved to the end of the bed. Standing, she made her way over to him and took him by the hand. Without a word, she led him into the bathroom, apparently wanting to talk somewhere that wouldn't bother Joe.

Good.

She pushed the door closed behind them with her foot. He rested against the marble counter and just as he opened his mouth to speak, she moved between his legs and took his face in her hands. He stopped as she stared into his eyes. His body responded; the hungry look she was giving him meant only one thing.

Leaning in, he took her lips and slipped his hands around her waist, pulling her hard against him so she could tell exactly how she made him feel. He wanted her, *had* wanted her from the moment she had come back into his life, but now she was on the cusp of walking back out.

Oh, the irony. It was an incredibly painful thing to have a life filled with contradictions.

As badly as he wanted to take this time and make every part of her body quake with ecstasy, he questioned it. Things were likely to change, permanently, between them if they opted for this road. If he chose to take her, here and now, it would be making the choice to keep her forever. But there was no way of knowing if she was in the same place or same frame of mind. Maybe she wanted to have one last night together.

He wanted to stop their kiss, to pull back and talk. But from her feverish pitch, if he pulled away now, it would only lead to a full stop. He couldn't run the risk of her thinking that his questioning their situation was any sort of rejection.

Summer was and had always been his everything, even when they hadn't been together.

She tasted like trepidation and excitement, mixed with the sweet and salty flavor of her lips. He'd always loved the way she tasted.

Reaching up, she ran her fingers through his hair, guiding his mouth closer, savoring their kiss.

"Take me," she said, not even bothering to stray from their kiss.

Damn, she was so damn hot.

He flipped her around so that she was pressed against the counter and then lifted her onto the cold stone. She gasped as he slid down her pants and her warm flesh pressed against the marble. He smiled, taking a certain amount of joy in the fact that she was having such a medley of sensations. He couldn't have planned it better. She was the kind of woman who needed every sense thrumming to really enjoy lovemaking.

He got down on his knees in front of her and kissed her skin, starting at her ankle and slowly working all the way up her inner thigh to the soft, satiny fabric of her panties. She tasted just as good as her lips. As he gently ran his fingers under the edge of her underwear, she lifted her hips and he slipped them down her legs, exposing her fully to the air.

He pulled her closer to the edge of the counter as he gave her a greedy grin. Reaching up, he unbuttoned her shirt, pulling it off her shoulders as he kissed where the fabric had just rested. He slipped his hands behind her back and undid the clasp of her bra with two fingers. Thankfully, that part was easier than he had remembered. He smiled as he edged the black straps down and exposed her dark pink nipples to the air. They were as hard as he was and he pulled one into his mouth. She arched beneath his kiss, groaning as he made her nipple grow impossibly harder. He flicked his tongue against her hard nub.

He ached for her as she moved against him. "I hope I'm still as good at some things as you remember," he said, releasing her from his torturous kiss.

She answered with a lusting, seductive smile. "I'm sure you are. If anything, I bet it's like fine wine and it's gotten better with age, just like the rest of you."

He ran his hands along her thighs toward the point where they met. He grazed her most sensitive bit, making her shudder. "That's what I think of you calling me 'old.' You won't do it again, will you?" He pressed his fingers inside her as he spoke, eliciting only a nod as a moan rippled from her throat.

His mouth went to the place his fingers had been and her moan grew louder. This was one of those moments he wished he could make last forever. He loved watching her as she threw her head back, her glistening hair falling down her back. Her lips had grown pinker, the same shade as her nipples.

He took his time, savoring her sweetness and the way she writhed as he worked her over. Yes, if he spent his entire life in this position, he would have considered it a life well spent. It didn't take long until a series of quakes and shudders took over her body and she cried out.

He hadn't lost his touch. She held out her hands, motioning for him to stand, apparently unable to find the words.

Her eyes were glazed. This was just how he liked her—well sated, to the point that all she could do was smile and relax.

And yet, instead of relaxing, Summer reached down and opened his belt buckle, kissing his neck as she slowly unzipped his pants. With her mouth moving against his neck, he could barely register everything she was doing to him, but he soon found his pants on the floor and her putting on a condom and directing him into her.

She leaned back as he slowly moved inside her.

"Damnnnn…" he groaned, barely able to think about anything besides how she felt against him.

He had spent many nights since their breakup imagining moments and memory-makers like these, with her back pressed against the mirror and her ass on the countertop of a hotel bathroom, but they all paled in comparison to the reality.

Though she had been thoroughly satisfied once, Mike knew he held the power to send her there again. If this was going to be the last time they'd ever be together, he wanted to give her the best she could get. Maybe, if he was lucky, she would think about him after she left and use him in the same way he had spent so many nights thinking about and using her.

He pressed deep into her, hitting the depth of her but giving her more. She moaned, the sound full of pleasure and tipped with the sweetness he knew could bring her to the edge once again. Slowly, he worked in and out, until her nectar ran heavy…she was close.

Summer grabbed his hand and pressed it against her mouth as she finished. The sensation of her arching and quaking against him made it impossible to hold back. Together they found what they had both been missing.

Chapter Eighteen

There were perfect moments in her life, but last night had been one of the best. Mike had always been an incredible lover, but he was even better than she had remembered.

What was even sweeter was that after their love-making, they had gone to bed together. He had wrapped her in his arms and she had slept better than she had in years. Joe had even managed to sleep through the night, which was a miracle in and of itself.

But now came the time to say goodbye.

Every part of her hurt with the thought of leaving her boys. And there was nothing she hated more than goodbye. Hawaiians had it right, using only one word—*aloha*—interchangeably for both hello and goodbye. With only one word, you were reminded at the moment of parting of how good it had felt to say hello. It was almost a reminder that soon enough the person you loved so much would be coming back into your life. But maybe goodbye really was the better word here; she could make no promises of return. She could only hope.

Mike held Joe in his lap, rocking him gently as he fed him a bottle. Joe was gazing over at her as he guzzled the liquid, but she couldn't help but notice the way he refused to turn his head away from her. The look in his young, innocent eyes didn't make her leaving any easier.

"I'm sorry, little guy. Mama has to go. I love you." She looked at Mike and their eyes met. "And I love you too," she said, regretting that she hadn't said it before in the last few days.

She wished she had found a better moment to tell Mike how she was really feeling, but this would have to do. At least he wouldn't be left wondering if she felt the same as he did. Sure, they could only have a long-distance relationship right now, but hopefully the future brought something different.

She couldn't believe she was leaving.

But she had to go before this got any more difficult than it already was.

One more kiss. She walked over and ran her hand over Joe's soft, downy hair, trying to take this one last chance to memorize the way his hair felt, just like she was touching a passing cloud. Leaning in, she gave him a soft kiss and took in his baby smell.

She looked up at Mike. "I hope you know that you are going to do great. Since the beginning, I have always known you would be the world's greatest dad. And husband." Her voice cracked.

He took her hand, his warmed by the baby, and pulled her lips to his. "I love you, Summer. When things go back to normal, I would be honored if you would consider being my wife."

In her wildest dreams she wouldn't have thought something like that would happen—her walking out seconds after Mike promised her forever.

Though her thoughts briefly moved to the past, she really only cared about this moment and the hope that rested at her fingertips, fingertips that had just brushed against the clouds and now rested in the radiant warmth of Mike's sunny touch.

"And I would be thrilled if you would allow me the honor of taking you as my husband." She kissed him, lacing her lips against his with a delicate promise. "With or without a piece of paperwork, the ceremony, and a party... I thee wed."

"And I thee wed, Mrs. Spade."

She took his face in her hands. "Mr. Spade." She rested her forehead against his, letting this simple touch in this complicated moment be all that she needed to solidify the bond and promise that had been so long in coming between them.

"Forever, you will be mine and I will be yours." Mike put his hand on hers, cupping them together against the stubble on his face.

She gave him one last kiss, letting her lips linger on his for a moment too long, a moment that allowed the tears to start to well in her eyes. Instead of turning away, blocking him from seeing how she truly felt, she let him look upon her...let him see that this was harder than anything before.

"I'm sorry I have to do this. I'm sorry I have to leave," she said, trying to keep herself from sobbing.

"Baby, you know I understand. But you have to know that you are not leaving forever. Only for right now, and Joe and I will be waiting for you when you get back."

"Where are you going to take him?" she asked.

"Once I know you're safe, I'll take him back to the STEALTH compound. When you are ready, you can come there too. We can plan a real wedding. Get every kind of flower you can dream of and have a ceremony at the bottom of a rolling mountainscape. We could do it this month, have the world covered in snow. Do a winter wedding."

She knew he was talking of all this in an attempt to give her a moment to collect herself and to think about something other than the pain she was feeling, and she loved him more for it. He had always known how important it had been to her that she stay strong, and he also knew how it was a battle she often lost—and he loved her through it all.

"I'd love a winter wedding. Red flowers, gray mountains, white snow." She could see the landscape in her mind's eye. Yes, it would have been beautiful. "All I'd want is me, you, Joe and a witness. Something simple."

"All I want is you." He smiled.

"I'll start planning," she continued. "I have a feeling that I may have a great deal of free time on my hands when I get to Kirtland. They will probably have me doing a bit of training, but—"

Mike's phone buzzed, cutting her off.

He looked down, surprise registering on his features. "Kevin is outside. He is waiting."

She wouldn't even bother to wonder how or when Kevin had gotten Mike's number and tracked her down to this hotel, but he must have figured out that she didn't have hers with her and just as quickly gotten a bead on them.

There was no more time for softness, no more time for goodbyes. There was only the harsh, bitter, wintery reality that waited for her outside.

"Have a good flight." Mike let go of her and re-settled Joe's bottle for him. "Let me know when you make it and that you got there safely. Okay?"

She nodded as she turned, grabbed her bags, and walked out. Looking back, she gave him one more wave as the door to her world closed behind her.

KEVIN WAS SITTING in a blue pickup outside the lobby's front doors. He was scowling at his phone, looking annoyed. This was going to be either the longest or the shortest trip ever. Only time would tell.

Summer knocked on the window. He looked up and motioned for her to get in, but the annoyed look on his face didn't lessen. Throwing her bags in the back seat, she climbed up into the front passenger seat of the truck and buckled in.

Kevin didn't say anything as he put the truck into gear and pulled away from the hotel. The air was heavy with angst, but she wasn't sure if it was coming from her or from Kevin. Though she wanted to ask him about the day's plans, she didn't dare speak. This was his show, and he had been kind enough to offer her a safe harbor.

They drove for five minutes before he finally cleared his throat. "What did you learn?"

She slid him a sideways look, trying to figure out exactly what kind of answer he was looking for from such a cold, no-lead question. "I'm sorry?" she asked. "What do you mean?"

"What has this exercise taught you?" He repeated the question in the same monotone voice.

"Exercise?" What was he talking about?

Kevin didn't say anything as he pulled up to the gates of Malmstrom Air Force Base, flashed the guard his ID and answered a few questions before the gates were opened and they were waved through.

He remained silent as her mind whirled, trying to make sense of Kevin's question. Was he implying that what had happened to her—Joe's kidnapping... the code exchange—all of it had been some sort of training exercise?

She had to have heard him wrong. He couldn't have possibly put her and her child in danger in an attempt to teach her something... Or had it been to test her?

She didn't understand. She couldn't understand. Her thoughts came in short, fast bursts.

If Kevin was using this to teach her something, he was a total jerk. Who would use her child? If that was what he was willing to do, then she wasn't sure this job and the people she worked for were the kinds of people she wanted to be associated with.

Anger oozed from her pores. She could kill the man sitting next to her. "How in the hell do you sleep at night?"

He frowned as he looked over at her. "What?"

"Are you telling me that all of this was your doing? That your people *took my son*? That you staged all this?" She tried to find the words threatening to melt together in her fiery rage. "How did you get Ben to go along with this nonsense?"

Kevin slowed as he drove through the base, toward the airfield. "First, I don't know who Ben is or what you think he's gone along with. Second, it wasn't my idea to do things this way. I have to answer to a boss, as well, and I was just told what to do and how to do it. I didn't agree to kidnapping Joe, but your friend Mike made it all too easy for our contractors to get their hands on your boy."

How dare he blame this on Mike. He hadn't done anything she wouldn't have done. "You had to have given them the okay. No one would just take a child."

"I don't have to answer your questions, but given the circumstances and how all of this has unfortunately played out, I will make an exception in telling you that those men—the contractors who took Joe—paid the price for coloring outside the lines. For this training exercise, they were given strict instructions to watch you and to learn your potential weaknesses while you dug into Mike for information about Rockwood. However, they jumped the gun. Both have been released from their contracts with DARPA."

"And that is all to say nothing about how you played me," she seethed. "You made me feel like I wasn't going to get Joe back. You manipulated me into playing their stupid game."

Oh crap. What have I done by bringing Mike into this?

"Is Mike in trouble?" she asked.

"Don't you think you should be more concerned about your own welfare, given the fact that you brought an unauthorized person into your work with the DTRA?" Kevin asked.

"If Ben hadn't threatened me, and if your people hadn't taken *our son*, I would have never gone to Mike for help. You forced me into a position where I had no allies. What little I told him was limited to what he needed to know. You can hardly hold that against me."

Kevin stared at her for a long moment. "Who is Ben and how did he threaten you, exactly? Are you talking about your ex from your days in Rockwood?"

She shrugged. Was this another of Kevin's sick, twisted games?

She should quit. Right here, right now. Then she should storm off in righteous indignation.

And yet she sat in the passenger side of his truck, unmoving. What did that mean? Was she just stunned so greatly that she was afraid to move? Did she love her job so much that she didn't want to walk away?

The thoughts rippled through her, creating an

electric buzz that cascaded into her fingertips and down to her toes. The sad and beautiful truth was that she did…she loved this job. She loved being a part of something bigger than herself. Something that stopped the bad guys from getting their hands on the weapons that could and would hurt so many.

Summer didn't agree with the methods those above them had used to make her prove her worth and dedication, but if they had thought her unworthy based on their findings, she wouldn't be sitting where she now sat. "Did I pass? Are these stupid training exercises over?" she asked, wary but hopeful.

"We booked you on a private plane to take you back to the main office. What do you think?" Kevin asked, giving her a wink. "I seriously do hope you know that I am in your corner with all of this. I went to bat for you."

She couldn't bring herself to say thank you, but from the tired look in Kevin's eyes she didn't think he was looking for her gratitude. If anything, he looked apologetic. That response was something she could appreciate and understand.

She gave him a tight nod in simple recognition of his efforts.

"When we get to Kirtland," he continued, "we have set up a series of secondary training exercises with several other candidates."

"Candidates?" she asked, taken aback. "For what?"

"Thanks to your work, the DTRA has been work-ing on a new program that focuses solely on world-wide IGS through nanotechnology. We would like you to take a lead role in the project and to help create a better training program so we never find ourselves in a similar situation."

"Am I being bought off?" she challenged. "Am I getting this opportunity because someone above you feels guilty or is it actually because of merit?"

Kevin chuckled. "I wish I had the answers for you, but you know as much as I do in this case. If I were you, though, I wouldn't look this gift horse in the mouth. This is the one chance you may get to advance and also get to be at home with Joe more often. After all this, do you really want to continue being a field agent?"

"No." There was no hesitation in her response, no need to think about her choices or about what she wanted. "I want to be with Joe. I can't put him into a situation like this ever again. And while I'm sure the DTRA would never intentionally put him into danger again, I can see now that, no matter what steps I take or don't take, being an agent will put him in harm's way. That's unacceptable. And as much as I love my job and I want to continue working with this group, I can't take that kind of risk with my child."

Kevin nodded understandingly. "If I'm being completely honest, I'm surprised you are still sitting here with me and are willing to go. I would get it if you turned in your ID and quit. What happened… was a cluster of mistakes and I'm embarrassed that it even happened like it did."

"From what you've said, none of this was your

fault. You had a job. I had a job. We had to play our parts. I don't like it. I don't like what happened. It is unacceptable and I will be requesting that there be follow-up investigations and procedural changes, but what better way to do this than from a job inside? I can be the change so no one ever has to go through anything remotely close to what I've had to go through."

"That is one hell of a great perspective," Kevin said, nodding his head in appreciation. "I can tell you right now that it is that attitude and outlook on life that got you this job and is going to make you successful in years to come. I'm proud to be a part of your journey, but remember me and the benefits of this organization when you are looking down from your seat in Congress. Okay?"

Summer laughed. The last thing she wanted to do was to be involved even more deeply in politics than she already was. Even though she wasn't going to continue as a field agent and would instead move into more of a political sector role, it didn't mean that she wanted to become a dealmaker. And yet, who knew what the future would bring? Life had a way of throwing curveballs that were so strong and swift, no one could catch them; all they could do was try to get out of the way and hope for the best.

The plane's crew was standing out by the stairs, waiting.

This was her last chance to say no and walk away. But as quickly as the idea came to her mind, it disappeared. Summer's life was about to change in ways she struggled to imagine. To top things off, she could be the wife and the mother she had always wanted to be.

In this moment of change, she could have it all.

"Ready?" Kevin asked, motioning to the waiting aircraft.

She reached back and grabbed her bags, then opened the passenger-side door. "I'm as ready as I'm ever going to be."

Stepping out of the truck, she slung her bags over her shoulder and closed the door. As the door slammed, there was a crack. That sound. She knew that sound. Without thinking, she hit the ground.

Someone was shooting at them.

As her body hit the cold, snow-laden tarmac, the bags she had been carrying rolled off her back. She felt heat radiate up from her core. Reaching down, her fingers prodded her side. There was something warm and wet. As she touched the spot, it felt as if a fire was racing through her, setting her nerves ablaze with pain.

There was a whizzing sound as another round pierced the air just above her head.

Someone wasn't just shooting at *them*; they were shooting at *her*.

Someone wanted her dead. And based on the fact that they were still shooting even though she'd been hit, they wouldn't stop until they were sure she was dead.

Chapter Nineteen

After having dropped off Joe with Jessica, Mike sat at the top of the offset from the airfield. He scoped from the hill and waited as Kevin and Summer sat in the truck. He could tell they were talking and as the minutes passed, some of the anger on Summer's face had started to diminish and was replaced with what he could best assume was relief.

His assault rifle with its long-range scope was perched on its bipod, concealed under the little makeshift tent he'd propped up around him using a borrowed sheet from the hotel. He'd also used all the white-and-black clothes he could find in an effort to blend into the snowy landscape.

She didn't need to know he was watching, that he couldn't stand by and just let her leave with a man and a team who had put them all in danger. Yeah, right.

If anything, given how much she knew him, it was a bit of a surprise that Summer hadn't been watching in the rearview mirror for him the entire way to the base. Sure, he'd had to borrow a late-model Buick from the hotel parking lot, but if things went right and she got on the plane without any sort of event, he would have the car and sheets back to the hotel before anyone even knew they were missing.

Getting onto the base had been more of a trick, but given his and STEALTH's levels of clearance, it had only taken a minute for the guard to make the necessary calls and for the gates of Malmstrom to open to him. Not for the first time, Mike found himself chuckling at the limited levels of security. Yes, he had a reason, the clearances, and a right to be on the base, but it struck him as darkly funny that he had to be there to provide cover and security for his fiancée.

He watched as the passenger door of the pickup opened and Summer stepped out, carrying her bags. As she closed the door, there was the rip of a round through the still Montana air.

What in the hell?

Using his rifle, he scoped the area around the base, looking for the shooter or shooters. Was there someone else, someone camouflaged like him, waiting just outside the perimeter of the airfield?

He looked over at Summer; she was lying on the ground. Her fingers came up from her side and, even from two hundred yards away, he could make out the distinct red color of fresh blood.

Someone had shot her.

How dare someone hurt the woman he loved.

Mike moved his sights in the direction in which he thought he'd heard the shot originate from. As he did, he caught a muzzle flash from the corner of his eye as the shooter fired off another round.

People on the base began to move quickly, like ants, as they started to make sense of what was happening and the reality that they were coming under fire from some unknown assailant.

There was another shot, but this time Mike spotted the little orange blaze that appeared to erupt from a blanket of snow. Whoever was shooting at Summer was using cover, just like him. If the shooter had been just a little more careful in the planning, Mike might not have even seen the flash. He had gotten lucky.

Hopefully, he would continue to be.

Mike took aim, carefully making calculations for distance and wind speed as he lined up his target. He would likely only get one easy shot. If he missed, the shooter would be on the run at a distance, making it even more of a challenge to neutralize the threat.

He had to get this right.

Clear.

Take the shot.

He found his mark, a tiny black spot in the midst of white where he assumed the shooter's head would be. He aimed small, centering his sights on the tiny black spot. His finger moved inside the guard and he felt the steely, cold ridges of the trigger. He applied even, steady pressure, making sure not to engage the sympathetic movement in his hand and interfere with his shot.

Precision. This was all about precision.

This was the moment he had trained for his entire adult life. He was the protector, the keeper of hearts, the man in the shadows, and the hero no one could identify—if he did things right.

The shot didn't surprise him, he had known it was coming, but the pressure he'd applied to the trigger had been so steady and even that when the firing pin hit the primer, it nearly shocked him. The suppressor did its job as the round moved down the barrel and cut into the air. There was only the dull *pew* sound as the round left and sought its target.

He stared as the bit of copper found that little black dot in which he had been aiming.

Damn. Sometimes he was good.

He smiled at the shot.

But had he neutralized the threat?

The firing stopped. No more rounds filled the air from where the shooter had been lying and taking aim at Summer.

Just to be sure he'd done his job, Mike sent another round downrange, striking just a few millimeters to the right of his first aim. He wouldn't stop firing until he knew his target was no longer a threat.

Crimson blood started to seep out onto the ground near his target. The shooter moved to stand, pushing the cover he had been lying under up and off. The man was dressed in white-and-black camouflage of the more commercial type, like the kind someone would buy at a sporting goods store.

The camo outfit was unmarred, but as the man moved, blood poured from his neck, just below his ear. He reached up and put his hand to his neck, applying pressure. But it was too late and Mike watched as he sank to his knees, his blood pressure lowering and starting to fail as the life seeped from him.

If the dude thought he could attempt to hurt or kill the woman Mike loved…well then, the dude deserved to die. No one hurt Summer. Never again.

Mike grabbed his gear and slipped away, hoping to remain unseen and the man in the shadows.

He rushed back to the borrowed Buick and made to leave the air base. He didn't want to have to answer questions about the shooting and find himself in some kind of court battle. He wasn't that kind of man. No, he was the kind who snuck in, did his job, and snuck out. And, for all intents and purposes, that was exactly what he needed to do now, as well.

Except, he couldn't bear the thought of knowing Summer was wounded, bleeding, and he was about to start running in the other direction. No. He couldn't leave her. He had to get down there, make sure she was okay and help stabilize her until the medics arrived. This being a military base, it wouldn't take long.

He drove toward the airfield, stopping far enough away from the strip that he wouldn't get pulled over by the airmen starting to swarm the area. Getting out, he stepped into a snowdrift. A USAF Security Forces airman rushed toward him, his hands raised. "You need to stop right there, sir."

That was not going to work on him, not now, with Summer waiting. "The woman out there on the tarmac, she is my…" He paused for a half second as he thought of exactly what he should call her so that the airman would be most willing to let him go to her. "She's going to be my wife. I need to get to her. To make sure she's okay. She's been shot."

"I'm more than aware she has been shot, sir." The airman looked in the direction of Summer, where another airman was kneeling beside her. He had his hands on her stomach, applying what looked like a compress to stop the bleeding.

"Look, I need to get to her. Please. I'm begging you."

"Sir, we have an active shooter situation, I recommend that you get back into your car and leave the area before someone takes a shot at you."

Mike tried to cover his smirk. "I can guarantee that the threat here is neutralized. I saw your shooter go down. If you let me go to her, I'll take you to the man's body."

The Security Force airman—known as an SF— turned away, clicking on his handset to likely call in to his fellow officers. Before the man could turn back, Mike sprinted past him toward Summer. The airman reached out and tried to grab him, but he swiveled around his grasp and charged away.

Mike slid to a stop on the icy tarmac next to her, the SF close at his heels. "Summer. Summer, I'm here. Are you okay?" he asked, taking her hand.

She looked up at him, shock in her eyes, but thankfully it looked as though it was only shock at seeing him as a smile crossed over her features. "Mike? What? How?"

He sent her a wicked smile in return and tipped his head in the direction of the shooter. "You couldn't believe that for one second I was going to let you get out of my sight. At least not until I knew you were safe and tucked away on the plane."

Her smile quaked as the airman holding the bandage moved. "Sir, you need to back up. The medics will be here at any moment, sir."

"I will leave as soon as she tells me to and not a second sooner."

"Sir, if you don't move away from this woman, I will be forced to place you under arrest."

The SF behind him piped up. "You should be under arrest already."

He had broken several laws and would be willing to break several more if it meant taking care of her, but for now he needed to get these guys to just back off. "I'm not trying to cause a scene. Really. I just—"

"Excuse me, gentlemen. Please leave my friend here alone." There was the crunch of footsteps on the tarmac as Kevin walked toward them.

"But, sir—" the SF standing behind Mike said.

"Lieutenant, it would be in your best interest— should you wish to continue your career in the air force—if you simply busy yourself with finding out where the medics are. If they are not on-scene in the next minute, I will make sure all of you find yourselves in your CO's office getting the ass-chewing of a lifetime before the day is out. Do you understand me?"

Mike wasn't sure what had happened, or who was behind the pulling of the trigger, but it appeared as though the culprit wasn't Kevin. A certain amount of relief filled him; at least their enemy wasn't the man standing directly in front of them.

Before he made up his mind about their safety, Mike glanced at Summer, giving an inquisitive look between she and Kevin.

Summer dipped her head. "It's all good. I'll explain later though." She was breathing hard as though it hurt to take in too deep a breath. "Is the shooter down?"

Mike gave her a tight nod. "The threat has been neutralized. No other shooters in the area. But I haven't been able to make a positive ID on the trigger puller."

"I need to know," she said. She tried to move to standing, but the airman held his hands in place and she winced in pain.

"We will know who was behind this soon enough. For now, we just need to get you to the hospital and get you stitched up. We don't want you bleeding all over the place," he teased, trying to keep her from thinking about anything but taking care of herself.

"This is not going to make wedding dress fittings any easier, you know."

He laughed.

Behind him, the medics rolled up and, parking on the tarmac, rushed over. He was pushed out of the way as they took Summer's vitals. Her blood pressure was high, but her oxygen sat levels were normal and the bleeding appeared to be under control. From what he could see as they pulled up her shirt, the bullet had traveled clean through—entering from the back just to the side of where her kidney would be and exiting out of her side. He was no doctor, but based on the looks of the wound, she would be okay. Especially as the bleeding was no longer an issue.

"Sir, you said you would show us where to find the body of the shooter," the SF who had chased after him said, pulling him back to the world outside of Summer.

"Absolutely." Mike nodded. "Summer, babe, you going to be okay for a minute?" he asked over the sounds of the medics asking her questions and talking to each other.

Summer looked up at him and smiled. "I'll be fine. Nothing more than a little flesh wound."

He glanced at the medic, who gave him a slight nod, reaffirming her assessment. "She'll be okay. We just need to get her to the infirmary and get her fixed up."

"Don't take her anywhere without letting me know first. She is not going to the infirmary without me, understand?"

The medic gave him a glove-handed thumbs-up. "You got it, sir."

The SF put his hand on Mike's shoulder, the action too invasive, and Mike turned out of it. The airman was just doing his job, but he always hated to be touched—except when it came to Summer.

"The guy was up this way," Mike said, motioning toward the snowy patch where his victim had been. He started to pick his way through the airmen and medics milling around the area, some talking on handsets and others talking with one another as they all seemed to be trying to make sense of what had happened. He didn't envy their job.

"Did you see what happened to him?" the SF asked, following him off the tarmac and into the knee-deep mounds of snow shoveled off in preparation for a day of flights.

Mike shrugged, noncommittal. "I saw him take the shot that hit Summer. Then I saw a splatter of blood when a projectile hit him."

"Did you see who made the shot on the assailant?" the SF asked, his breathing heavy as he stumbled over a chunk of ice and was forced to recover.

Mike held back a chuckle; he felt bad for the kid, he really did. Here he was, trying to do his job and investigate a shooting and not look like a total idiot, and not only was Mike going to have to keep some key details from him, now the kid was tripping around in front of his main eyewitness.

"You all right there, Lieutenant?"

The soldier straightened his uniform and put his hand down to his sidearm as though afraid that somehow it would slip from its holster. "Yep, just fine." He cleared his throat uncomfortably. "You were saying…about the shooter?"

Mike smiled as he looked away and up toward the man who lay dead in the snow. "I didn't see who shot him, or where it came from. Sorry."

"But you are sure the shooter was neutralized."

He nodded. He knew death. "Absolutely."

The young SF continued asking questions until Mike spotted the little knoll. "The guy is up there," he said, pointing just ahead of them. "You can make out his footsteps behind in the snow, just there."

The SF pressed by him, hurrying toward the body. He knelt as he reached the man and pulled back his balaclava. Even from where he stood, based on the chunk of missing flesh, Mike could tell the man was deceased. And yet the SF pressed his fingers to the man's neck. As he did, the man's head rolled slightly, exposing his face.

Mike knew that face. He had seen it outside Summer's apartment complex when the man had been sneering at him. It was Ben.

Mike had been right all along. Ben must have been stalking them, watching as they went around Great Falls together. If Mike had just trusted his gut from the first moment and kicked the guy's ass, this shooting would have never had to happen.

Now he was going to have to tell Summer she had been gunned down by her ex.

But why? Summer had told him that Ben had threatened them because of their being together, that he was just a crazy ex, but could this have also had something to do with Rockwood? Had they found out that she was, in fact, a double agent?

On the ground, by the tip of Mike's boot, lay a cell phone.

There was the crunch of footsteps in the snow behind them and Mike turned. Kevin was making his way next to him and, as he stopped, he looked down and also spotted the cell phone in the snow.

"Whoever made this shot was one hell of a marksman." Kevin winked in his direction.

What was that wink supposed to mean? Kevin couldn't have known that Mike had made the kill shot, and yet he definitely seemed to. Son of a...

"Yeah," the SF said, looking back at Mike from over his shoulder. "Considering I barely saw this dude until I walked right up on him, the shooter had to have known what he was doing."

"I'm sure it was probably one of your guards. You airmen are on the money when it comes to this kind of thing. You should be proud. I know I am," Kevin added.

"Well, sir, it will take a bit of investigative work, but I'm sure we will figure out exactly what happened here in just a few days. Either of you recognize this man?" the SF asked.

Kevin looked over at Mike then looked down at the cell phone, but not before Kevin gave him an understanding smirk. "I think ID'ing him shouldn't be too challenging. In fact, I would appreciate it if you could pull together as much about this incident as possible in the next day or two. I will talk to your superior officers and let them know that my team will be handling it from there."

"Yes, sir." The SF looked slightly excited at the prospect of working for someone as high up in the Pentagon as Kevin. He turned back to the body, snapping a few pictures with his cell phone as though he was trying to capture the entire scene.

Kevin had definitely just lit a fire under the lieutenant.

Mike looked over at Summer's boss, who was still staring at him as though he was trying to read his mind. After a moment, Kevin knelt and pretended to tie his shoe. Checking to make sure the SF's back was turned to them, Kevin picked up the cell phone and stuffed it into his back pocket. He stood and gave Mike a tip of the head.

"Do you know this man?" Kevin asked, his voice barely above a whisper so that only Mike could hear.

He nodded. "It's Ben, Summer's ex."

Kevin sighed. "Good. Good. I'm glad he has been taken out of the situation. I have reason to believe he was feeding information to his organization about Summer."

"Well, he won't be anymore," Mike said with a devilish smile.

"Good job out here," Kevin said. "You handled this situation very well. I can only imagine what you've gone through, you know, with everything with your son."

Mike didn't know if he should admit his role to this man, but clearly there were to be no secrets between them when it came to this shooting. "Just doing my part."

As he looked over at the dead man and stared at Ben's lifeless eyes, Mike couldn't help but be the slightest bit pleased. He didn't like having to pull the trigger and take down a bad man, but he had told Ben that if he wasn't careful, he would put him in his grave. The man had been warned to not mess with Summer. Ben had made a choice to mess with the dragon, and he had called the flames.

"If there's anything I can do, as a token of my gratitude for your service to this country, all you have to do is let me know," Kevin said, extending his hand in gratitude.

Mike shook his hand as a sense of ease filled him. "Actually, there is something that Summer and I wanted, maybe when things cool off a bit, you can help..."

Chapter Twenty

It felt good to rest. A week had passed and she had been answering a flurry of phone calls with requests for interviews from a variety of newspapers and military journals, but as soon as she had mentioned their constant badgering to Kevin, all had come to a stop. In fact, besides hearing from Mike when he'd run to the commissary and a couple of messages from Kevin, she hadn't gotten any other phone calls. It had been pure bliss and she had finally just been able to enjoy her alone time with Joe and Mike. Things hadn't been this quiet in her life in a long time. Not saying she wanted to be shot again, but she was thoroughly enjoying the peace.

Mike was busying himself around the kitchen of their house in Kirtland, making her a sandwich. After she had been seen by the doctors at the infirmary and cleared, they had gotten on the plane and headed to New Mexico where Kevin had instructed them they were to stay until the things with Rockwood were cleared and she had finished up the training she needed for her new job—once she healed of course.

The house they had been assigned was far nicer, and larger, than her apartment in Great Falls. Everything had been prefurnished and all she and Mike had had to do was hang their clothes in the closets and set up a crib for Joe. Everything was nice, far nicer than she had expected to find on a military base. Thankfully, Kevin had gotten them into the officer's housing. Aside from seeing her friend Jessica, she had to admit that she held no desire to go back to Montana for a while.

Mike sauntered out of the kitchen, carrying a tray complete with two Tylenol and her antibiotics. Setting it down beside her on the couch, he made sure the blanket was wrapped neatly around her feet. "You need anything else? I'm gonna go check on Joe. He has got to be getting up from his nap soon." He motioned in the direction of the second bedroom.

"Kevin said he is going to stop by soon. I think he is worried about me." She smiled up at him. "He sounded *off*, maybe excited or something."

"Kevin's a good guy. You are lucky to have a boss like him," Mike offered. "If you want, I can give you guys a few minutes to talk without me around."

"No, he mentioned that he wanted to talk to you." She gave him a questioning glance.

Ever since the shooting, Mike and Kevin had been up to something, she could feel it, and yet both had kept their lips shut. She had to assume it was about his role in the shooting. No one had spoken of his killing Ben. It was almost as if it had been silently agreed upon by all involved that Ben's death would be one of those things swept under the rug.

No doubt, Kevin had had to pull a lot of strings for something like that to happen since the death had occurred on a military base. But the last thing DTRA would have wanted was additional scrutiny on their organization and what they had been doing on an airfield in the middle of a freezing Montana day.

Mike walked to the bedroom and there were the sounds of him talking to Joe as he obviously began a diaper change. After a few minutes, he came out to the living room with Joe cradled in his arm. When her son saw her, a giant grin erupted on his face and he threw out his arms, reaching for her.

"Oh, someone is happy to see Mama after his big nap," Mike said, bringing him over to her and placing him in her arms. He reached behind him and pulled out a bottle. "I made him this too. I bet he's hungry."

She took the bottle. Being a dad suited Mike more than she could have ever expected. Though he had struggled, putting the first diaper on and receiving a little shower, things since then had clicked into place between her two boys. They were made for one another. There was nothing better than watching them together, Mike talking to him and Joe laughing at his father.

Love filled her as Joe gripped the bottle, shoved it into his little mouth and started suckling. It had taken some major hardships and fighting to get here, but she finally had the life she had always wanted. The only thing that could have made it better was if she could have really and truly called Mike her husband.

It had been awkward when they had been shown the house and asked the status of their relationship. Neither had really known what to say until Mike had finally told the man they were engaged. Of course, the man had instinctively glanced at her naked ring finger, but had been gracious enough not to mention the lack of a ring.

There was a knock on the door.

She moved to stand, but Mike stopped her with a wave. "I got it."

He walked over to the door and opened it for Kevin. The warm desert air swept into the living room, with it came the scent of earth and dried grass.

"How are you feeling?" Kevin asked, walking inside and closing the door behind him. "All healed up and ready to hit the ground running?"

Summer put her hand to her side where the stitches were itching. "Maybe a few more days before I go for a run. But I should be ready to get back to training shortly. When were you thinking?"

Kevin glanced over at Mike and they exchanged looks, but she didn't understand why.

"I don't want you to worry about going back to work just yet. I'll let you know when we want you. In the meantime—" Kevin paused, walking over and sitting on the edge of the chair across the room from her "—I wanted to let you both know, in person, that we have analyzed Ben's phone. As it turns out, we found text messages and emails between him and his fellow members of Rockwood—one of which was a senator's son. He had been sent to take you out if he found that you were working for the feds."

"So, they didn't know anything about me stealing the codes from ConFlux?" she asked, silently begging for that fear to be unfounded.

"No," Kevin said, shaking his head. "You are in the clear. They had just feared that you were a double agent, as I said. When Ben learned the truth, he did tell his team. They ordered him to put you down."

"So, she is never going to be safe as long as Rockwood knows she was working for you?" Mike asked.

A lump rose in her throat.

Kevin rubbed his hands together. "Just for now. As such, we are going to keep you here until we can neutralize their organization. However, in the meantime, we will start building Summer an alternative identity. I have no doubts that we can make you, Summer—for all intents and purposes—disappear."

Disappearing and being safe at the expense of giving up her public identity was just fine. There was little to her life as it was, besides Joe and Mike.

"That's fine."

Kevin smiled and some of his nervousness evaporated. "Good. I was hoping you wouldn't find that to be too much of a problem."

Summer nodded. "I know we've had our issues, but you've gone above and beyond in making up for it. I appreciate all your hard work."

Kevin gave a slight dip of the head in acknowledgment. "You know how I feel about what happened, so I appreciate that you guys are taking all of this in stride."

Mike walked over and put his hand on her shoulder. "Here, let me take Joe." He lifted Joe from her as he kept feeding.

Kevin slapped his knees and smiled up at Mike. "Enough of that. Now, you said you weren't up for a run, but are you up for a small walk, Summer?" Kevin gave Mike a wink.

Mike held out his hand to help her to standing. Gently, she rose.

"What are you guys up to?" she asked, grinning.

"Well, no pressure or anything, but Kevin and I have been working on a bit of a surprise for you."

She cocked her head slightly. "And this would be?"

Mike smiled. "Come outside and see." He interlaced their fingers and pulled her toward the door. Opening it, she walked out.

There, along the road, someone had lined the sidewalk with red roses. The yard was covered in fake snow and at the end of the walk there was a string quartet playing "Ave Maria." The song brought tears to her eyes.

She really did love that song, and hearing it and knowing just how much work Mike must have gone through to make this happen in a place he had never been after changing his life basically overnight for her and Joe...it was all just *perfect*.

He walked her out into the middle of the fake snow and dropped down to one knee, Joe still in his arm. "Summer Daniels, I have loved you from the first moment we met. Our lives have been like our love and filled with ups and downs, but truly what they were meant to be. I want to be the best father and husband in the world and build a life with you that is filled with all the laughter and happiness that our lives will allow. Summer, will you marry me?" He reached into his back pocket and pulled out a gold band with a princess-cut solitaire at its center.

It was simple and beautiful as it gleamed in the New Mexico sun.

"Yes, Mike Spade." She covered her mouth with her hand and excitedly bounced from one foot to the other as he slipped the ring onto her finger.

But he didn't get up. "Now, since we are engaged…and before either of us can run, be chased, or slip away—" He looked over toward the quartet, where a man was standing with a Bible in his hand "I propose that we get married right here, right now."

He reached into his other back pocket and pulled out two rings, a simple gold band for each of them.

Summer squealed in agreement.

For once, everything was perfect. No more fear. No more running. They were safe and the stars had aligned. She and Mike would have their forever love and they could officially and legally become a family—the greatest gift she could have wished to receive.

For once in her life, she had everything—honor, love, and family.

* * * * *

SPECIAL EXCERPT FROM

⬥ HARLEQUIN
INTRIGUE

*LAPD detective Jake McAllister has his work cut out
for him trying to identify and capture a serial killer
hunting women. The last thing he needs is victims' rights
advocate Kyra Chase included on his task force. He
senses trouble whenever she's around, and not just to
his hardened heart. It also seems she might have a very
personal connection to this most challenging of cases…*

Keep reading for a sneak peek at
The Setup,
*the first book in A Kyra and Jake Investigation,
from Carol Ericson.*

He'd recognize that voice anywhere, even though he'd
heard it live and in person just a few times and never
so…forceful. He believed her, but he had no intention
of letting her off the hook so easily.

He raised his hands. "I'm LAPD Detective
Jake McAllister. Are you all right?"

A sudden gust of wind carried her sigh down the trail
toward him.

"It…it's Kyra Chase. I'm sorry. I'm putting away my
weapon."

Lowering his hands, he said, "Is it okay for me to
move now?"

"Of course. I didn't realize… I thought you were…"

"The killer coming back to his dump site?" He flicked on the flashlight in his hand and continued down the trail, his shoes scuffing over dirt and pebbles. "He wouldn't do that—at least not so soon after the kill."

When he got within two feet of her, he skimmed the beam over her body, her dark clothing swallowing up the light until it reached her blond hair. "I didn't mean to scare you, but what are you doing here?"

"Probably the same thing you are." She hung on to the strap of her purse, her hand inches from the gun pocket.

"I'm the lead detective on the case, and I'm doing some follow-up investigation."

"Believe it or not, Detective, I have my own prep work that I like to do before meeting a victim's family. I want to have as much information as possible when talking to them. I'm sure you can understand that."

"Sure, I can. And call me Jake."

Don't miss
The Setup *by Carol Ericson,*
available April 2021 wherever
Harlequin Intrigue books and ebooks are sold.

Harlequin.com

HIEXP0321

Get 4 FREE REWARDS!

We'll send you 2 FREE Books plus 2 FREE Mystery Gifts.

Harlequin Intrigue books are action-packed stories that will keep you on the edge of your seat. Solve the crime and deliver justice at all costs.

FREE Value Over $20

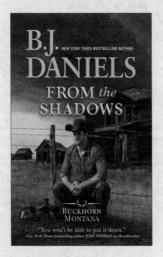

SPECIAL EXCERPT FROM

H

HQN

Everyone says the hotel Casey Crenshaw inherited is haunted. She wants to sell it as quickly as possible, but Finn Faraday is throwing a wrench into her plans. He's determined to figure out what happened at the hotel years ago, but Finn and Casey will soon discover that digging into the past can be dangerous...

Read on for a sneak preview of From the Shadows, *the second book in the Buckhorn, Montana series by* New York Times *bestselling author B.J. Daniels.*

Chapter One

Finn lay on the dusty floor of the massive, old and allegedly haunted Crenshaw Hotel and extended his arm as far as it would go into the dark cubbyhole he'd discovered under the back stairs. A spider web latched on to his hand, startling him. He chuckled at how jumpy he was today as he shook the clinging strands from his fingers. He had more to worry about than a few cobwebs. Shifting to reach deeper, his fingers brushed over what appeared to be a notebook stuck in the very back.

Megan Broadhurst's missing diary? Had he finally gotten lucky?

The air from the cubbyhole reeked of age and dust and added to the rancid smell of his own sweat. He should have been used to all of it by now. He'd spent the past few months searching this monstrous old relic by day. At night, he'd lain awake listening to its moans and groans, creaks and clanks, as if the place were mocking him. *What are you really looking for? Justice? Or absolution?*

What he hadn't expected, though, was becoming invested in the history of the place and the people who'd owned it, especially the new owner—who would be arriving any day now to see the hotel demolished. Casey Crenshaw had inherited the place after her grandmother's recent death. Word was that she'd immediately put it up for sale to a buyer who planned to raze it.

Finn had been looking for a place to disappear when he'd heard about the hotel, which had been boarded up and empty for the past two years. He'd known it would be his last chance before the hotel was destroyed. It had felt like fate as he'd gotten off the bus in Buckhorn and pried his way into the Crenshaw. He'd been in awe of the hotel, which had once been popular with presidents, the rich and famous, and even royalty, the moment he stepped inside.

He'd only become more fascinated when he'd stumbled across Anna Crenshaw's journals. That was why he felt as if he already knew her granddaughter, Casey. He was looking forward to finally meeting her.

His fingers brushed over the notebook pages. He feared he would only push it farther back into the dark space or worse, that its pages would tear before he could get good purchase. Carefully he eased the notebook out.

This was the first thing he'd found that had been so well hidden. He hoped that meant it was the diary that not even the county marshal and all his deputies had been able to find.

Don't miss
From the Shadows *by B.J. Daniels,*
available March 2021 wherever HQN books
and ebooks are sold.

HQNBooks.com

PHBJDEXP0321